THE
ICE PRINCE

THE
ICE PRINCE

BY

SANDRA MARTON

GW31819397

First published in Great Britain 2011
by Mills & Boon, an imprint of Harlequin (UK) Limited.
Large Print edition 2011
Harlequin (UK) Limited, Eton House,
18-24 Paradise Road, Richmond, Surrey TW9 1SR

© Sandra Marton 2011

ISBN: 978 0 263 22241 8

CHAPTER ONE

THE first time he noticed her was in the Air Italy VIP lounge.

Noticed? Later, that would strike him as a bad joke. How could he not have noticed her?

The fact was, she burst into his life with all the subtlety of a lit string of firecrackers. The only difference? Firecrackers would have been less dangerous.

Draco was sitting in a leather chair near the windows, doing his best imitation of a man reading through a file on his laptop when the truth was he was too sleep-deprived, too jet-lagged, too wound up to do more than try to focus his eyes on the screen.

As if all that weren't enough, he had one hell of a headache.

Six hours from Maui to Los Angeles. A two-hour layover there, followed by six hours more to New York and now another two-hour layover that was stretching toward three.

He couldn't imagine anyone who would be happy at such an endless trip, but for a man accustomed to flying in his own luxurious 737, the journey was rapidly becoming intolerable.

Circumstances had given him no choice.

His plane was down for scheduled maintenance, and with the short notice he'd had of the urgent need to return to Rome, there'd been no time to make other arrangements.

Not even Draco Valenti—*Prince* Draco Marcellus Valenti, because he was certain his ever-efficient PA had resorted to the use of his full, if foolish, title in her attempts to make more suitable arrangements—could come up with a rented aircraft fit for intercontinental flight at the last minute.

He had flown coach from Maui to L.A., packed in a center seat between a man who oozed over the armrest that barely separated them and an obscenely cheerful middle-aged woman who had talked nonstop as they flew over the Pacific. Draco had gone from polite *mmms* and *uh-huhs* to silence, but that had not stopped her from telling him her life story.

He had done better on the cross-country flight to Kennedy Airport, managing to snag a suddenly available first-class seat, but again the person next to him had wanted to talk, and not even Draco's stony silence had shut him up.

For this last leg of his journey, the almost four thousand miles that would finally take him home, he had at the last minute gone to the gate and, miracle of miracles, snagged two first-class seats—one for himself, the other to ensure he would make the trip alone.

Then he'd headed here, to the lounge, comforted by the hope that he might be able to nap, to calm down, if nothing else, before the confrontation that lay ahead.

It would not be easy, but nothing would be gained by losing control. If life had taught him one great lesson, that was it. And just as he was silently repeating that mantra, trying to focus on ways to contain the anger inside him, the door to the all but empty first-class lounge swung open so hard it banged against the wall.

Cristo!

Just what he needed, he thought grimly as the pain in his temple jumped a notch.

Glowering, he looked up.

And saw the woman.

He disliked her on sight.

At first glance, she was attractive. Tall. Slender. Blond hair. But there was more to see and judge than that.

She wore a dark gray suit, Armani or some similar label. Her hair was pulled back in a low, no-nonsense ponytail. A carry-on the size of a small trunk dangled from one shoulder, a bulging briefcase from the other.

And then there were the shoes.

Black pumps. Practical enough—except for the spiked, sky-high heels.

Draco's eyes narrowed.

He'd seen the combination endless times before. The severe hairstyle. The businesslike suit. And then the stilettos. It was a look favored by women who wanted all the benefits of being female while demanding they be treated like men.

Typical. And if that was a sexist opinion, so be it.

He watched as her gaze swept across the lounge.

There were only three people in it at this late hour. An elderly couple, seated on a small sofa, their heads drooping, and him. Her eyes moved over the sleeping couple. Found him.

And held.

An unreadable expression crossed her face. It was, he had to admit, a good face. Wide set eyes. High cheekbones. A full mouth and a determined chin. He waited; he had the feeling she was about to say something…and then she looked away and he thought, *Bene.*

He was not in the mood for making small talk; he was not in the mood for being hit on by a woman. He was not in the mood for any damned thing except being left alone, returning to Rome and dealing with the potential mess that threatened him there, and he turned his attention back to his computer as her heels tap-tapped across the marble floor to the momentarily deserted reception desk.

"Hello?" Impatience colored her voice. "Hello?" she said again. "Is anyone here?"

Draco lifted his head. Wonderful. She was not just impatient but irritable, and she was peering over the desk as if she hoped to find someone crouched behind it.

"Damn," she said, and Draco's lips thinned with distaste.

Impatient. Irritable. And American. The bearing, the voice, the *me-über-alles* attitude—she might as well have had her passport plastered to her forehead. He dealt with Americans all the time—his main offices were in San Francisco—and while he admired the forthrightness of the men, he disliked the lack of femininity in some of the women.

They tended to be good-looking, all right, but he liked his women warm. Soft. Completely female. Like his current mistress.

"Draco," she'd breathed last night after he'd joined her in the shower of the beachfront mansion he'd rented on Maui, lifted her into his arms and taken her while the water beat down on them both. "Oh, Draco, I just adore a man who takes charge."

No one would ever take charge of the woman at the reception desk, now tapping one stiletto-clad foot with annoyance, but then, what man would be fool enough to want to try?

As if she'd read his thoughts, she swung around and stared around the room again.

Stared at him.

It lasted only a couple of seconds, not as long as when they'd made eye contact before, but the look she gave him was intense.

So intense that, despite himself, he felt a stir of interest.

"So sorry to have kept you waiting," a breathless voice said. It was the lounge hostess, hurrying toward the reception desk. "How may I help you, miss?"

The American turned toward the clerk. "I have a serious problem," Draco heard her say, and then she lowered her voice, leaned toward the other woman and began what was clearly a rushed speech.

Draco let out a breath and dropped his eyes to his computer screen. That he should, even for a heartbeat, have responded to the woman only proved how jet-lagged he was.

And he had to be in full gear by the time he reached Rome and the situation that awaited him.

He was accustomed to dealing with difficult situations. In fact, he enjoyed resolving them.

But this one threatened to turn into a public mess, and he did not countenance public any-things, much to the media's chagrin. He did not like publicity and never sought it.

He had built a financial empire from the ruins of the one his father and grandfather and count-less great-great-grandfathers had systematically plundered and ultimately almost destroyed over the course of five centuries.

And he had done it alone.

No stockholders. No outsiders. Not just in his financial existence. In his world. His very private world.

Life's great lesson *numero due.*

Trusting others was for fools.

That was why he'd left Maui after a middle-of-the-night call from his PA had dragged him out of a warm bed made even warmer by the lush, naked body of his mistress.

Draco had listened. And listened. Then he'd cursed, risen from the bed and paced out the bedroom door, onto the moon-kissed sand.

"Fax me the letter," he'd snapped. "And every-thing we have in that damned file."

His PA had obliged. Dressed in shorts and a

T-shirt, Draco had read through it all until the pink light of dawn glittered on the sea.

By then he'd known what he had to do. Give up the cooling trade winds of Hawaii for the oppressive summer heat of Rome, and a confrontation with the representative of a man and a way of life he despised.

The worst of it was that he'd thought he'd finished with this weeks ago. That initial ridiculous letter from someone named Cesare Orsini. Another letter, when he ignored the first, followed by a third, at which point he'd marched into the office of one of his assistants.

"I want everything you can find on an American named Cesare Orsini," he'd ordered.

The information had come quickly.

Cesare Orsini had been born in Sicily. He had immigrated to America more than half a century ago with his wife; he had become an American citizen.

And he had repaid the generosity of his adopted homeland by becoming a hoodlum, a mobster, a gangster with nothing to recommend him except money, muscle and now a determination to acquire something that had, for centuries, belonged to the House of Valenti and now to him, Prince Draco Marcellus Valenti, of Sicily and Rome.

That ridiculous title.

Draco didn't often use it or even think it. He found it officious, even foolish in today's world. But, just as his PA would have resorted to using it in her search for a way to get him from Hawaii to Italy, he had deliberately used it in his reply to the American don, couching his letter in cool, formal tones but absolutely permitting the truth— *Do you know who you're dealing with? Get the hell off my back, old man*—to shine through.

So much for that, Draco had thought.

Wrong.

The don had just countered with a threat.

Not a physical one. Too bad. Draco, whose early years had not been spent in royal privilege, would have welcomed dealing with that.

Orsini's threat had been more cunning.

I am sending my representative to meet with you, Your Highness, he had written. *Should you and my lawyer fail to reach a compromise, I see no recourse other than to have our dispute adjudicated in a court of law.*

A lawsuit? A public airing of a nonsensical claim?

In theory, it could not even happen. Orsini had no true claims to make. But in the ancient land that was *la Sicilia,* old grudges never ended.

And the media would turn it into an international circus—

"Excuse me."

Draco blinked. Looked up. The American and the lounge hostess were standing next to his chair. The American had a determined glint in her eyes. The hostess had a look in hers that could only be described as desperate.

"Sir," she said, "sir, I'm really sorry but the lady—"

"You have something I need," the American said.

Her voice was rushed. Husky. Draco raised one dark eyebrow.

"Do I, indeed?"

A wave of pink swept into her face. And well it might. The intonation in his words had been deliberate. He wasn't sure why he'd put that little twist on them, perhaps because he was tired and bored and the blonde with the in-your-face attitude was, to use a perfectly definitive American phrase, clearly being a total pain in the ass.

"Yes. You have two seats on flight 630 to Rome. Two first-class seats."

Draco's eyes narrowed. He closed his computer and rose slowly to his feet. The woman was tall, especially in those ridiculous heels, but at six foot three, he was taller still. It pleased him that she had to tilt her head to look at him.

"And?"

"And," she said, "I absolutely must have one of them!"

Draco let the seconds tick by. Then he looked at the hostess.

"Is it the airline's habit," he said coldly, "to discuss its passengers' flying arrangements with anyone who inquires?"

The girl flushed.

"No, sir. Certainly not. I don't—I don't even know how the lady found out that you—"

"I was checking in," the woman said. "I asked for an upgrade. The clerk said there were none, and one word led to another and then she pointed to you—you were walking away by then—and she said, 'That gentlemen just got the last two first-class seats.' I couldn't see anybody with you and the clerk said no, you were flying alone, so I followed you here but I figured I should confirm that you were the man she'd meant before I—"

Draco raised his hand and stopped the hurried words.

"Let me be sure I understand this," he said evenly. "You badgered the ticket agent."

"I did not badger her. I merely asked—"

"You badgered the hostess here, in the lounge."

The woman's eyes snapped with irritation.

"I did not badger anyone! I just made it clear that I need one of those seats."

"You mean you made it clear that you want one."

"Want, need, what does it matter? You have two seats. You can't sit in both."

She was so sure of herself, felt so entitled to whatever she wanted. Had she never learned that in this life no one was entitled to anything?

"And you need the seat because…?" he said, almost pleasantly.

"Only first class seats have computer access."

"Ah." Another little smile. "And you have a computer with you."

Her eyes flashed. He could almost see her lip curl.

"Obviously."

He nodded. "And, what? You are addicted to Solitaire?"

"Addicted to...?"

"Solitaire," he said calmly. "You know. The card game."

She looked at him as if he were stupid or worse; it made him want to laugh. A good thing, considering that he had not felt like laughing since that damned middle-of-the-night phone call.

"No," she said coldly. "I am not addicted to Solitaire."

"To Hearts, then?"

The hostess, wise soul, took a step back. The woman took a step forward. She was only inches away from him now, close enough that he could see that her eyes were a deep shade of blue.

"I am," she said haughtily, "on a business trip. A last-minute business trip. First class was sold out. And I have an important meeting to attend."

This time it was her intonation that was interesting.

He had not bothered shaving; he had taken

time only to shower and dress in faded jeans and a pale blue shirt with the sleeves rolled to his elbows, the top button undone. He wore an old, eminently comfortable pair of mocs and, on his wrist, the first thing he'd bought himself after he'd made his first million euros—a Patek Phillipe watch for no better reason than the first own he'd owned he had stolen and, in a fit of teenage guilt, had a day later tossed into the Tiber.

In other words he was casually but expensively dressed. A woman wearing an Armani suit would know that. He'd reserved two costly seats, not one. Add everything together and she would peg him as a man with lots of money, lots of time on his hands and no real purpose in life, while she was a captain of industry, or whatever was the female equivalent.

"Do you see why the seat is so important to me?"

Draco nodded. "Fully," he said with a tight smile. "It's important to you because you want it."

The woman rolled her eyes. "My God, what's the difference? The seat is empty."

"It isn't empty."

"Damnit, will someone be sitting in it or not?"

"Or not," he said, and waited.

She hesitated. It was the first time she had done so since she'd approached him. It made her seem suddenly vulnerable, more like a woman than an automaton.

Draco felt himself hesitate, too.

He had booked two seats for privacy. No one to disturb his thoughts as he worked through how to handle what lay ahead. No one with whom he'd have to go through the usual *Hello, how are you, don't you hate night flights like this one?*

He was not in the mood for any of it; if truth be told, he was rarely in the mood for sharing his space with others.

Still, he could manage.

He didn't like the woman, but so what? She had a problem. He had the solution. He could say, *Va bene, signorina. You may have the seat beside mine.*

"You know," she said, her voice low and filled with rage, "there's something really disgusting about a man who thinks he's better than everyone else."

The hostess, by now standing almost a foot away, made a sound that was close to a moan.

Draco felt every muscle in his body tighten. *If only you were a man,* he thought, and for one quick moment imagined the pleasure of a punch straight to that uptilted chin.....

But she wasn't a man, and so he did the only thing he could, which was to get the hell out of there before he did something he would regret.

Carefully he bent to the table where his laptop lay, turned it off, put it in its case, zipped the case closed, slung the strap over his shoulder. Then he took a step forward; the woman took a step back. Her face had gone pale.

She was afraid of him now. She'd realized she had gone too far.

Good, he thought grimly, even though part of him knew this was overkill.

"You could have approached me quietly," he said in a tone of voice that had brought business opponents to their knees. "You could have said, 'I have a problem and I would be grateful for your help.'"

The color in her face came back, sweeping over her high cheekbones like crimson flags.

"That's exactly what I did."

"No. You did not. You told me what you wanted. Then you told me what *I* was going to do about it." His mouth thinned. "Unfortunately for you, *signorina,* that was the wrong approach. I don't give a damn what you want, and you will not sit in that seat."

Her mouth dropped open.

Hell. Why wouldn't it? Had he really just said something so foolish and petty? Had she reduced him to that?

Get moving, Valenti, he told himself, and he would have…

But she laughed. Laughed! Her fear had given way to laughter.

His face burned with humiliation.

There was only one way to retaliate and he took it.

He closed the last inch of space between them. She must have seen something bright and icy-hot glowing in his eyes, because she stopped laughing and took another quick step back.

Too late.

Draco reached out. Ran the tip of one finger over her lips.

"Perhaps," he said softly, "perhaps if you had offered me something interesting in trade…"

He put his arms around her, lifted her into the leanly muscled length of his body and took her mouth as if it were his to take, as if he were a Roman prince in a century when Rome ruled the world.

He heard the woman's muffled cry. Heard the hostess gasp.

Then he heard nothing but the thunder of his blood as it coursed through his veins, tasted nothing but her mouth, her mouth, her sweet, hot mouth…

She hit him. Hard. A surprisingly solid blow to the ribs. The sting of her small fist was worth the rage he saw in her eyes when he lifted his head.

"Have a pleasant flight, *signorina,*" he said, and he brushed past her, leaving Anna Orsini standing right where he'd left her, staring at the lounge door as it swung shut behind him while she wished to hell she'd had the brains to slug the sexist bastard not in the side but right where he lived.

Where all men lived, she thought grimly as she

snatched up her carry-on and briefcase that had somehow ended up on the floor.

In the balls.

CHAPTER TWO

ANNA stalked through the crowded terminal, so furious she could hardly see straight.

That insufferable pig! That supermacho idiot!

Punching him hadn't been enough.

She should have called the cops. Had him arrested. Charged him with—with sexual assault....

Okay.

A kiss was not sexual assault. It was a kiss. Unwanted, which could maybe make it a misdemeanor...

Not that anyone would call what had landed on her lips *just* a kiss.

That firm, warm mouth. That hard, long body. That arm, taut with muscle, wrapped around her as if she were something to be claimed...

Or branded.

A little shudder of rage went through her. It *was* rage, wasn't it?

Damned right it was.

Absolutely, she should have done something more than slug him.

Where was the gate? Her shoulders ached from the weight of her carry-on and briefcase. Her feet hurt from the stilettos. Why in hell hadn't she had the sense to change to flats? She'd worn the stilettos to court. Deliberately. It had become her uniform. The tailored suit coupled with the spike heels. It was a look she'd learned worked against some of the high and mighty prosecutors who obviously thought a female defense counsel, especially one named Orsini, would be easy to read.

Nothing about her was easy to read, thank you very much, and Anna wanted to keep it that way.

But the shoes were wrong for hurrying through an airport. Where on earth was that gate?

Back in the other direction, was where.

Anna groaned, turned and ran.

By the time she reached the right gate, the plane was already boarding. She fell in at the end of the line of passengers shuffling slowly forward. Her hair had come mostly out of the tortoiseshell clip that held it; wild strands hung in her face and clung to her sweat-dampened skin.

Anna shifted her carry-on, dug into its front pocket, took out her boarding pass. Her seat was far back in the plane and, according to the annoyingly perky voice coming over the loudspeaker, that section had already boarded.

Perfect.

She was late enough so that the most convenient overhead bins would surely be full by the time she reached them.

Thank you, Mr. Macho.

The line, and Anna, moved forward at the speed of cold molasses dripping from a spoon.

He, of course, would have no such problem. First-class passengers had lots of overhead storage room. By now he probably had a glass of wine in his hand, brought by an attentive flight attendant who'd do everything but drool over her good-looking passenger, because there were lots of women who'd drool over a man who looked like that.

Tall. Dark. Thickly lashed dark eyes. A strong jaw. A face, a body that might have belonged to a Roman emperor.

And the attitude to go with it.

That was why he would have access to a computer outlet, and she would not....

Anna took a breath. No. Absolutely not. She was not going there!

Concentrate, she told herself. Try to remember what it said on those yellowed, zillion-year-old documents her father had given her.

Hey, it wasn't as if she hadn't read them....

Okay. She hadn't read them. Not exactly. She'd looked through them prior to scanning them into her computer, but the oldest ones were mostly handwritten. In Italian. And her Italian was pretty much confined to *ciao, va bene* and a handful of words she'd learned as a kid that wouldn't get you very far in polite company.

The endless queue drew nearer to the gate.

If only she'd had more time, not just to read those notes but to arrange for this flight. She'd have flown first class instead of coach, let her father pay for her ticket because Cesare was the only reason she was on this fool's errand.

Cesare could afford whatever ridiculous amount of money first class cost.

She certainly couldn't. You didn't fly in comfort on what you earned representing mostly in-digent clients.

And comfort was what first class was all about. She'd flown that way once, after she'd passed her bar exams and her brothers had given her a two-week trip to Paris as a gift.

"You're all crazy," she'd said, blubbering hap-pily as she bestowed tears and kisses on Rafe and Dante, Falco and Nicolo.

Plus, she'd flown on the private jet her brothers owned. Man, talk about flying in comfort...

"Boarding pass, please."

Anna handed hers over.

"Thank you," the gate attendant said. In, natu-rally, a perky voice.

Anna glowered.

Seven hours jammed into an aluminum can like an anchovy was not something to be perky about.

Not that she disliked flying coach. It was what real people did, and she had spent her life, all twenty-six years of it, being as real as possible.

Which wasn't easy, when your old man was a *la famiglia* don.

It was just that coach had its drawbacks, she

thought as she trudged down the ramp toward the plane. No computer outlets, sure, but other things, too.

Like that flight to D.C. when the guy next to her must have bathed in garlic. Or the one to Chicago, when she'd been sandwiched between a mom with a screaming infant on one side and a dad with a screaming two-year-old on the other.

"You guys want to sit next to each other?" Anna had chirruped helpfully.

No. They didn't. They weren't together, it turned out, and why would any sane human being want to double the pleasure of screaming kids trying their best to drive everyone within earshot to infanticide?

One of the flight attendants had taken pity on her and switched her to a vacant seat. To the *only* vacant seat.

Unfortunately, it was right near the lavatories.

By the time the plane touched down, Anna had smelled like whatever it was they piped into those coffin-sized closets.

Or maybe worse.

In essence, flying coach was like life. It wasn't always pretty, but you did what you had to do.

And what she had to do right now, Anna told herself briskly, was find a way to review her notes in whatever time her cranky old laptop would give her.

At last. The door to the plane was just ahead. She stepped through and somehow managed not to snarl when a flight attendant greeted her with a smiling *"Buona notte."*

It wasn't the girl's fault she looked as if she'd just stepped out of a magazine ad. Anna, on the other hand, knew she looked as if she had not slept or fixed her hair or her makeup in days.

Come to think of it, she hadn't.

Her father had dumped his problem on her twenty-four hours ago and she had not slowed her pace since then. A long-scheduled speech to a class of would-be lawyers at Columbia University, her alma mater. Two endless meetings. A court appearance, a desperate juggling of her schedule followed by a taxi ride to the airport through rush-hour Manhattan traffic, only to learn that her flight was delayed and that no, she could not upgrade her seat even though she'd realized during the taxi ride that she had to do so if she wasn't going to walk into the meeting in Rome without a useful idea in her head.

And on top of everything, that—that inane confrontation with that man…

There he was.

The plane was an older one, which meant the peasants had to shuffle through first and business class to get to coach. It gave her the wonderful opportunity to see him in seat 5A—all, what, six foot two, six foot three of him sitting in 5A, arms folded, long legs outstretched, with 5B conspicuously, infuriatingly empty.

Her jaw knotted.

She wanted to say something to him. Something that would show him what she thought of him, of men like him who thought they owned the world, thought women were meant to fall at their feet along with everybody else, but she'd already tried that and look where it had gotten her.

And, almost as if he'd heard her thoughts, he turned his head and looked right at her.

His eyes darkened. The thick lashes fell. Rose. His eyes got even darker. Darker, and focused on her face.

On her mouth.

His lips curved in a slow, knowing smile. *Remember me?* that smile said. *Remember that kiss?*

Anna felt her cheeks turn hot.

His smile tilted, became an arrogant, blatantly male grin.

She wanted to wipe it from his face.

But she wouldn't.

She wouldn't.

She wouldn't, she told herself, and she tore her gaze from his and marched past him, through first class, through business class, into the confines of coach where the queue ground to a halt as people ahead searched for space in the crowded overhead bins and stepped on toes as they shoehorned themselves into their designated seats.

"Excuse me," Anna said, "sorry, coming through, if I could just get past you, sir…"

At last she found her row and found, too, with no great surprise, that there was no room in the overhead bin for her carry-on. Which was worse? That she had to go four more seats to the rear before she found a place where she could jam it into a bin, or that she had to fight her way back like a salmon swimming upstream?

Or that the guy in the window seat bore a scary resemblance to Hannibal the cannibal, and the woman on the aisle was humming. No discernible melody. Just a steady, low humming. Like a bee.

Anna took a deep breath.

"Excuse me," she said brightly, and she squeezed past the hummer's knees, tried not to notice that part of Hannibal's thigh was going to be sharing her space, shoved her bulging briefcase under the seat in front of her and folded her hands in her lap.

It was going to be a very long night.

At 30,000 feet, after the usual announcement that it was okay to use electronic devices, she hoisted the briefcase into her lap, opened it, took out her laptop, put down the foldout tray, plunked the machine on it and tapped the power button.

The computer hummed.

Or maybe it was the woman on the aisle. It was hard to tell.

The computer booted. The screen came alive. Wasting no time, Anna searched for and found the file she needed. Clicked on it and, hallelujah, there it was, the most recent document, a letter from Prince Draco Marcellus Valenti to her father.

The name made her snort.

So did the letter.

It was as stiffly formal as that ridiculous name and title, wreathed in the kind of hyperbole that would have made a seventeenth-century scribe proud.

One reading, and she knew what the prince would be like.

Old. Not just old. Ancient. White hair growing from a pink scalp. Probably growing out of his ears, too. She could almost envision his liver-spotted hands clutching an elaborate cane. No, not a cane. He'd never call it that. A walking stick.

In other words, a man out of touch with life, with reality, with the modern world.

Anna smiled. This might turn out to be interesting. Anna Versus the Aristocrat. Heck, it sounded like a movie—

Blip.

Her computer screen went dark.

"No," she whispered, "no..."

"Yup," Hannibal said cheerfully. "You're outta juice, little lady."

Hell. Little lady? Anna glared at him. What she was, was out of patience with the male of the species...but Hannibal was only stating the obvious.

Why dump her anger on him?

Sure, she was ticked off by what had happened in the lounge, but her mood had been sour even before that.

It had all started on Sunday, after dinner at the Orsini mansion in Little Italy. Anna's mother had phoned the previous week to invite her.

"I can't come, Mom," Anna had said. "I have an appointment."

"You have not been here in weeks." Sofia's tone of reprimand had taken Anna straight back to childhood. "Always, you have an excuse."

It was true. So Anna had sighed and agreed to show up. After the meal her father had insisted on walking her to the front door, but when they were about to pass his study, he'd stopped, jerked his head to indicate that Freddo, his *capo* and ever-present shadow, should step aside.

"A word with you alone, *mia figlia,*" he'd said to Anna.

Reluctantly she'd let Cesare lead her into the study. He'd sat down behind his massive oak desk, motioned her to take a seat, looked at her for a long moment and then cleared his throat.

"I need a favor of you, Anna."

"What kind of favor?" she'd said warily.

"A very important one."

Anna had stared at him. A favor? For the father she pretended to respect for the sake of her mother but, in reality, despised? He was a crime boss. Don of the feared East Coast *famiglia.*

Cesare had no idea she knew that about him, that she and her sister, Isabella, had figured it out when Izzy was thirteen and Anna was a year older.

Neither could remember exactly how it had happened. Maybe they'd read a newspaper article. Maybe the whispers of the girls at school had suddenly started to make sense.

Or maybe it was their realization that their big brothers, Rafe, Dante, Falco and Nick, had struck out on their own as soon as they could and treated Cesare with cold disdain whenever they visited the mansion and thought the girls and their mother were out of earshot.

Anna and Izzy only knew that one day they'd suddenly realized their father was not the head of a waste management company.

He was a crook.

Because of their mother, they hadn't let on that they knew the truth. Lately, though, that was becoming more and more difficult. Anna, especially, was finding it hard to pretend her father's hands were not dirty, even bloody.

Do a favor, for a man like him?

No, she'd thought. No, she wouldn't do it.

"I'm afraid I'm incredibly busy, Father. I have a lot on my plate just now, and—"

He'd cut her off with an imperious wave of his hand.

"Let us be honest for once, Anna. I know what you think of me. I have known it for a very long time. You can fool your mama and your brothers, but not me."

Anna had risen to her feet.

"Then you also know," she'd said coolly, "that you're asking the wrong person for a favor."

Her father had shaken his head.

"I am asking the right person. The only person. You are my daughter. You are more like me than you would care to admit."

"I am nothing like you! I believe in the law. In justice. In doing what is right, no matter what it takes!"

"As do I," Cesare had said. "It is only that we approach such things differently."

Anna had laughed.

"Goodbye, Father. Don't think this hasn't been interesting."

"Anna. Listen to me, *per favore.*"

The *per favore* did it. Anna sat back and folded her arms.

"I need to see justice done, *mia figlia.* Done your way. The law's way. Not mine. And you are a lawyer, *mia figlia,* are you not? A lawyer, one who carries my blood in her veins."

"I can't do anything about being your daughter," Anna said coldly. "And if you need an attorney, you probably have half a dozen on your payroll."

"This is a personal matter. It is about family. *Our* family," her father said. "Your mother, your brothers, your sister and you."

Not interested, Anna wanted to say, but the truth was Cesare had piqued her curiosity.

What her father was now calling "our family" had never seemed as important to him as his crime family. How could that have changed?

"You have five minutes," she said after a glance at her watch. "Then I'm out of here."

Cesare pulled a folder of documents from a drawer and dumped them on the shiny surface of his desk. Most were yellowed with age.

Anna's curiosity rose another notch.

"Letters, writs, deeds," he said. "They go back years. Centuries. They belong to your mother. To her family."

"Wait a minute. My mother? This is about her?"

"*Sì*. It is about her, and what by right belongs to her."

"I'm listening," Anna said, folding her arms.

Her father told her a story of kings and cowards, invaders and peasants. He spoke of centuries-old intrigue, of lies on top of lies, of land that had belonged to her mother's people until a prince of the House of Valenti stole it from them.

"When?"

Cesare shrugged. "Who knows? I told you, these things go back centuries."

"When did you get involved?"

"As soon as I learned what had happened."

"Which was what, exactly?

"The current prince intends to build on your mother's land."

"And you learned this how?"

Cesare shrugged again. "I have many contacts in Sicily, Anna."

Yes. Anna was quite sure he did.

"So what did you do?"

"I contacted him. I told him he has no legal right to do such a thing. He claims that he does."

"It's difficult to prove something that happened so long ago."

"It is difficult to prove something when a prince refuses to admit to it."

Anna nodded.

"I'm sure you're right. And it's an interesting story, Father, but I don't see how it involves me. You need to contact an Italian law firm. A Sicilian firm. And—"

Her father smiled grimly.

"They are all afraid of the prince. Draco Valenti has enormous wealth and power."

"And you're just a poor peasant," Anna said with a cool smile.

Her father's gaze was unflinching.

"You joke, Anna, but it is the truth. No matter what worldly goods I have accumulated, no matter my power, that is exactly what I am, what I shall always be, when measured against a man like the prince."

Anna shrugged. "Then that's that. Game, set, match."

"No. Not yet. You see, I have one thing the prince does not have."

"Blood on your hands?" Anna said with an even cooler smile than before.

"No more than on his, I promise you that." Cesare leaned forward. "What I have is you."

Anna laughed. Her father raised his eyebrows.

"You think I am joking? I am not. His attorneys are shrewd, clever men. They are paid well. But you, *mia figlia*... You are a believer."

She blinked. "Excuse me?"

"You graduated first in your class. You edited the *Law Review*. You turned down offers from the best legal firms in Manhattan to join one that takes on cases others turn away. Why? Because you believe," Cesare said, answering his own question. "You believe in justice. In the rights of all men, not only those born as kings and princes."

His words moved her. He was right—she did believe in those things.

And though it shamed her to admit it, even to herself, it warmed her heart to hear of his paternal pride in her.

Maybe that was why she brought her hands together in slow, insulting applause.

"Quite a performance, Father," she said as she rose and started for the door. "You want to give up crime, you might consider a career on—"

"Anna."

"Dear Lord," she said wearily, "what is it now?"

"I have not been the father you wanted or the one you deserved, but I have always loved you. Is there not some part of you that still loves me?"

Such simple words, but they had changed everything. The shameful truth was that he was right. Somewhere deep in her heart she was still a sweet, innocent fourteen-year-old who loved the father she had once believed him to be.

So she'd gone back to his desk. Sat across from him. Listened while he told her that he had been fighting to claim the land. He had sent Prince Valenti letters that the prince had ignored. He had contacted lawyers, in Sicily where the disputed land lay and in Rome, where the prince lived. None would touch the problem.

"We cannot permit a man like Valenti to ride roughshod over us simply because he believes our blood is not the equal of his," Cesare said. "Surely you must see that, Anna."

She did. Absolutely, she did. The haves and the have-nots had always been at war, and there was always fierce joy in showing the haves that they could not always win.

"Do not do this for me," Cesare had said. "Do it because it is right. And for your mother."

Now, hurtling through the skies at 600 miles an hour, Anna asked herself for what was surely the tenth time if she'd been had.

She sighed.

The thing was, she knew the answer.

Her father was right about her. She hated to

see the rich and powerful walk over the poor and powerless. Okay, her father was hardly poor or powerless, but her mother's family had surely been both when the House of Valenti stole the land.

Besides, she'd given her word that she'd meet with this Italian prince, and she would.

Too bad she wasn't the slightest bit prepared for the meeting, but her father was right—she was a good lawyer, an excellent negotiator. She could handle this even if she didn't know all the details and facts.

What did any of that matter? This was the privileged prince against the poor peasant and, okay, her father wasn't poor or a peasant, but the principle was the same.

This prince, this Draco Marcellus Valenti, was an anachronism. He lived in an elegant past with no idea the rest of the world was living in the twenty-first century.

Like that guy in the VIP lounge who thought he owned the world, owned people…

And any woman he wanted.

He probably could.

Women, idiots that they were for good looks, undoubtedly fawned all over him.

But not her.

Not her, no matter how his mouth felt on hers, how his arms felt around her, how alive that one kiss had made her feel...

Ridiculous.

He'd kissed her for a purpose. To show her that he was male, and powerful, and sexy.

But did that impress her? *Ha,* Anna thought, and she put her head back and closed her eyes.

What was sexy about a man with a low, deep voice? With darkly lashed eyes that were neither brown nor gold, and a face that might have been carved by an ancient Roman sculptor? With a body so leanly muscular she'd felt fragile in his arms, and that was saying a lot for a woman who stood five foot eight in her bare feet.

What could possibly be sexy about being kissed like that, as if an absolute stranger had the power to possess her? To put his mark on her, as if she were his woman?

Anna shifted in her seat.

What if instead of slugging him, she'd wound

her arms around his neck? Opened her mouth to his? What would he have done?

Would he have said to her, *Forget that plane. That flight. Come with me. We'll go somewhere dark and private, somewhere where I can undress you, whisper things to you. Do things to you...*

A tiny sound vibrated in her throat.

She could almost feel it happening. The kisses. The caresses. And then, finally, he'd take her. She'd been with men. Sex was as much a woman's pleasure as a man's, but this would be—it would be different.

He would make her moan, make her writhe, make her cry out...

"Signorina?"

Make her cry out...

"Signorina. Forgive me for disturbing your sleep."

Anna's eyes flew open.

It was him. The man from the lounge. The man who had kissed her.

The man whose kiss she could still feel on her lips.

He was standing in the aisle, looking down at her. And the little smile on his beautiful mouth stole her breath away.

CHAPTER THREE

DRACO watched as the woman's eyes flew open.

Blue, just as he recalled, but to say only that was like saying that the seas that surrounded Sicily were blue.

Not so.

The colors of the Ionian Sea, the Tyrrhenian Sea, the Mediterranean were more than blue. And so were her eyes.

Not pale. Not dark. The shade reminded him of forget-me-nots blooming under the kiss of the noon sun along the Sicilian cliffs where he was reconstructing a place that he was sure had once been as magnificent as the view those cliffs commanded.

His gaze fell to her mouth. Her lips were parted in surprise. It was a very nice mouth. Pink. Soft. Enticing.

Draco frowned.

So what? The color of her mouth, of her eyes,

was unimportant. She could look like the witch in *Hansel and Gretel,* for all it mattered to him.

He'd made his decision based on what was right and what was wrong, not on anything else.

A man who could not see past his own ego was not a man deserving of life's riches. That had been another lesson of his childhood, learned by watching how men with power, with wealth, with overinflated ideas of their own importance thought nothing of trampling on others.

At the announcement that it was now permissible to use electronic devices, he'd put aside his glass of more-than-acceptable burgundy, thanked the flight attendant for handing him the dinner menu, plugged in his computer...

And thought, suddenly and unexpectedly, of the woman.

Yes, she had infuriated him, that arrogant, the-world-is-mine-if-only-you'd-get-out-of-my-way attitude...

But was his any better?

Half an hour or so of soul-searching—remarkable, really, when you considered that many of those who knew him would have insisted Draco

Valenti had no soul to search—and he'd decided he might have overreacted.

After all, first-class flying was comfortable. Not as comfortable as his own jet would have been but still, it was acceptable. Yes, his legs were long, his shoulders broad but still, the seat accommodated him.

You could have made do with the one seat, he'd found himself thinking.

As for not wanting someone next to him who would jabber away the entire time… That wouldn't be a problem. The reason the blonde wanted that vacant seat was that she had work to do.

In other words, she would keep to herself.

He would keep to himself.

No problem in that at all.

The bottom line? He'd been tired, grumpy and bad tempered. She'd been desperate, overeager and short-fused. Not a good combination under any circumstances, and in these particular circumstances, it had led to her being insulting and him being no better.

It was, he'd decided, an honest assessment

and once he'd made it, he'd risen to his feet and headed toward the rear of the plane.

"Something I can do for you, Your Highness?" the eager flight attendant had said as soon as she saw the direction he was taking.

"Yes," Draco had said crisply. "You can stop calling me 'Your Highness.'"

He'd softened the words with a quick smile as he moved past her. Then he'd walked and walked and walked, going from first-class luxury to business-class efficiency and, finally, through what he'd tried not to think of as a sardine tin until he'd figured he might just end up in Oz.

And then, at last, he'd spotted her. Her sun-kissed hair was like a beacon. And when her eyes opened, her lips parted, he almost smiled, imagining how delighted she would be at the sight of him....

Maybe not.

She was staring at him as if he were an apparition. If he'd given it any thought, and he hadn't, he'd have known his sudden appearance would take her by surprise.

Well, it had.

But the look on her face, the shock and amazement, told him that she was a woman people rarely took by surprise.

That he'd done so was a bonus.

He could see her struggling for words. That was nice to see, too. She certainly hadn't been at a loss for words earlier...except when he'd kissed her....

And that kiss had as little to do with this as the color of her eyes. This was a matter of human decency. Nothing more and nothing less.

"Sorry to have awakened you," he said politely.

She sat up straight and tugged down her skirt, which had ridden halfway up her thighs.

They were good thighs.

Actually, they were great.

Firm. Smooth. Lightly tanned to a sort of gilded bronze. Was she that color all over? Her hips. Her belly. Her breasts...

Damnit, he thought, and when he spoke again his tone had gone from polite to brusque.

"I said I'm sorry to have—"

"I wasn't asleep."

Probably not. Who could sleep, jammed between a woman who looked like a ticking time bomb's worth of neuroses and a guy with a look about him that reminded Draco of some movie character he couldn't place.

"And what are you doing here?"

Draco cleared his throat. This wasn't going quite the way he'd anticipated.

"I, ah, I've changed my mind."

"About what?"

Dio, was she going to make this difficult?

"About the seat. If you want it, it's yours."

Her eyes narrowed. "Why?"

Her tone was flat. Sarcastic. Was she playing to their audience? The guy to her right and the woman to her left were both watching him with the intensity of people viewing an accident on a highway.

So much for doing the right thing, Draco thought grimly, and met her slitted stare with one of his own.

"Why?" he snapped. "Because, fool that I am, I thought you might still prefer a first-class seat to—to this!"

"What's wrong with this?" the woman next to her demanded, and Draco threw up his hands and started back up the aisle.

"Wait!"

The cry carried after him. It was her, the blonde with more attitude than any one person, male or female, could possibly need.

A smart man would have kept walking, but Draco had already proved to himself that he wasn't being terribly smart tonight, so he stopped, folded his arms, turned…

And saw her hurrying toward him, that ridiculously lumpy briefcase swinging from one shoulder.

Despite himself, his mouth twitched.

What had become of all her crisp American efficiency?

The heavy case had tugged her suit jacket askew in a way he suspected Giorgio Armani would never approve; her golden hair had slipped free of its clasp. A shoe dangled from her fingers. In her rush to go after him, she'd apparently lost one of those high heels, which she'd managed to retrieve.

Those incredibly sexy high heels.

The thought marked the end of any desire to laugh. Instead, his eyes grew even more narrow. It was an indicator of his mood, and would have made any of his business opponents shudder.

"Well? What is it?"

"I—I—"

His gaze, as cold as frost on a January morning, raked over her.

"You what?"

It was, Anna thought, an excellent question. How did you admit you'd made a mistake? Not in judging this man. He was as cold, as self-centered, as insolent as ever—but that wasn't any reason to have rejected his offer.

Never mind that she couldn't think of a reason he'd made it, or that sitting next to him all the way to Rome would be the equivalent of choking down more humble pie than any one human being should have to consume.

Only an idiot would refuse gaining access to a spot where she could plug in her computer... and, okay, incidentally combine that with a seat that lacked the psycho bookends.

"I am waiting," he growled, that accent of his growing more pronounced by the minute.

Anna swallowed. Hard. The first bite of crow did not go down easily.

"I—I accept your apology."

He laughed. Laughed, damn him! So did someone else. Anna looked around, felt her face blaze when she realized their little drama was proving more interesting than books or magazines to what looked like this entire section of the plane.

"I did not apologize. I will not apologize."

She drew closer. He was inches away. Once again she had to tilt her head to look up at him, the same as she'd had to in the lounge an eternity ago. It was just as disconcerting now as it had been then, and suddenly she thought, *He's going to kiss me again, and if he does—if he does...*

"What I did was offer you the empty seat beside mine." His mouth twisted. "The one you groveled for a little while ago."

"I did not grovel. I would never grovel. I—I—"

Anna fell silent. She didn't know where to look. There was nowhere that was safe, given the choice between his dark, hard eyes and the attentive faces of their audience.

"Jeez, lady, are you nuts? You tell him you'll take the seat or I will," a male voice said, and somebody snickered. "Yes or no, lady? Last chance."

Anna glared. It was a toss-up who she despised more—her father for putting her in this untenable position or this…this arrogant idiot for putting her in this situation.

"You are," she said, her voice shaking, "a horrible, hideous man."

His eyelids flickered. "I take it that's a yes," he said, and he swung away from her and headed briskly up the aisle.

Anna did the only thing that made sense.

She fell in behind him and followed him to the front of the plane.

An hour later Anna turned off her computer, closed it and put it away.

So much for going through the document file.

She'd read and read, switched screens and made notes, and she still didn't have a true grasp of what was happening.

No.

She had a grasp, all right.

She was about to step into a pile of doggy-doo, two centuries old and a mile high.

There was a piece of land somewhere in Sicily that either belonged to her mother or belonged to a prince. None of the papers Anna had seen proved ownership; none even hinted at it.

Unless the papers written in Italian said something different, the documents Cesare had given her proved nothing beside the fact that her father had sent several letters to the prince.

The prince had sent only one that really mattered.

It was a note written by one of his lackeys on a sheet of vellum that weighed almost much as her computer, and it took half a dozen paragraphs to say, basically, "Go away."

The one certainty was her father's insistence that the royal House of Valenti had stolen the land in question. And how could that be possible? Anna asked herself tiredly. She didn't know much about what her father called the old country, but she knew enough to be certain that peasants didn't argue with princes.

For all she'd learned, she might as well still be back in coach, without access to her computer.

And without access to the man seated on the aisle seat beside her.

Anna gave him a covert glance.

Access was the wrong word to use. He had not looked at her or spoken to her since they'd sat down. He had a computer on his lap, too, and it was the only thing that claimed his attention.

That was fine.

The hell it was.

Calmer now, she could look at him and admit that he was a beautiful sight. That chiseled, masculine face. That hard body. Those strong-looking hands, one lightly wrapped around his computer, the other working its touch pad...

She knew what his hands felt like.

Back in the lounge, he'd grasped her shoulder. Here, he'd put his palm lightly on the small of her back, guiding her into the window seat. His touch had been impersonal then.

What if he touched her differently?

Not that automatic, you-first thing men did, but a stroke of those long, tanned fingers. A caress of that powerful hand.

Anna frowned, shifted in her seat.

Such nonsense!

He wasn't her type and she wasn't his. He'd like girlie women. Pliable in nature, eager to please, the kind who'd do whatever it took to make a man happy.

She was none of that.

"Prickly," a guy she'd dated a couple of times had called her.

"Difficult," another had claimed.

"Tough as nails," her brothers said, with pride.

Yes, she was.

How else did a woman get to make it in a world dominated by men, or endure growing up in a household where your mother walked two paces behind your father? Metaphorically, of course, but still...

Back to peasants and princes. And the man next to her. And the simple fact that in this situation he was the prince. Not because of their different seating arrangements but because he'd done something gracious and she...

She had not.

Would a simple *thank you* have killed her?

No. It would not have.

Was it too late to say the words now? *It's never too late to say something nice,* she could almost hear her sister, Izzy, saying. Okay. She wasn't sweet like Iz—she never would be—but she could try.

"Finished already?"

She blinked. He was looking at her, a hint of a smile on his lips.

Anna cleared her throat. "Yes."

"Didn't find what you wanted on your computer?"

She shook her head. "I only wish."

"Same here." He closed the cover of his and put it away. "I'm going to a meeting that will almost surely be a complete waste of time."

"Sounds like my story." She gave a little laugh. "Don't you just hate that kind of thing?"

"I despise it," he said, nodding in agreement. "There's nothing worse than having to sit across the table from a guy who can't figure out he's absolutely not going to accomplish anything."

"Exactly. It's so useless." Anna sighed. "Actually, what I'd like to do is walk into my meeting and say, 'Okay, this is pointless. I'm going to turn around and go home and if you have half a brain, so will you.'"

He chuckled. "Yes, but if the idiot really had half a brain, he wouldn't be there, eating up your time in the first place."

Anna grinned. "Exactly."

"That's life, isn't it? Things don't always work out as one expects."

"No, they don't." She hesitated. It was the perfect segue, and she took it. "Which brings me to offering my thanks for this seat. I should have said it sooner, but—"

"Yes," he said, "you should have."

"Now, wait a minute…"

He laughed. "Just teasing. This was my fault, too. I overreacted when you first asked for the seat. How about we call it even? I'll apologize if you will."

Anna laughed, too. "You're not a lawyer, are you?"

He gave a mock shudder. "*Dio,* no. Why do you ask?"

"Because you have a way with words."

"It's what I do," he said, smiling. "I'm a negotiator." What better way to describe fashioning deals that made him millions and millions of dollars and euros? "So, do we have a truce?"

He held out his hand. Anna took it—and jerked back. An electric current seemed to flow from his fingers to hers.

"Static electricity," she said quickly. "Or something."

"Or something," he said, and all at once his voice was low and husky.

Their eyes met. His were dark, deep, fathomless. Anna felt her heartbeat stutter. *I'm tired,* she thought quickly. *I must be terribly tired or everything wouldn't seem so—so—*

"Would you like to see the wine list?"

It was the flight attendant, her smile perfect, her voice bright and bubbly, though Anna had to give her credit for not having reacted to the sight of a refugee from coach slipping into the cabin an hour or so before.

"Champagne," said the man still holding her hand, his gaze never leaving hers. "Unless you'd rather have something else?"

"No," Anna said quickly. "No, champagne would be lovely."

"Lovely," he said, and Anna wondered why she'd ever thought him cold or arrogant.

They drank champagne. In flutes. Glass flutes, not plastic. Switched to red wine, also in glasses, when dinner was served—served on china, with real flatware and real linen napkins.

Being in first class wasn't bad.

Neither was being with such a gorgeous stranger.

He ordered for them both. Normally Anna would have bristled at a man assuming he could order for her, but tonight it seemed right.

Everything seemed right, she thought as they ate and talked. Conversation flowed easily, not about anything important, just about the weather they'd left behind in New York, how it would compare to the weather they'd find in Rome, about where he lived—in San Francisco, overlooking the bay, he said. And where she lived—in Manhattan, on the lower east side.

For all of that, they didn't exchange names.

That seemed right, too.

There was something exciting about hurtling through the night at six hundred plus miles an hour, laughing and talking and having dinner with a man she didn't know and would never see again.

Anything was possible, Anna thought after their dishes had been whisked away and the cabin lights were dimmed. Absolutely anything, she thought, looking at him, and a faint tremor went through her.

"Are you cold?"

"No," she said quickly. "I'm fine."

"Tired, then."

"No. Really..."

"Of course you're tired. I'm sure your day has been as long as mine. In fact, I'm going to put my seat back. You'll do the same."

That tone of easy command made Anna laugh. "Do you ever ask a woman what she wants, or do you simply tell her?"

Their eyes met. Her heart did a little stutter step.

"There are times when there is no need to ask," he said softly.

Heat swept through her. *Get up,* she thought. *Get up and go back to your own seat in the rear of the plane.*

But she didn't.

He reached out. Leaned across her. She caught her breath as he pressed the button that eased her seat all the way back.

"Close your eyes, *bellissima*," he whispered. "Get some sleep."

She nodded. Closing her eyes, pretending to sleep was probably a good plan. No reason to tell him that she never, ever was able to sleep on a plane….

When she woke, the cabin was almost completely dark.

And she was cocooned in warmth.

Male warmth.

Somehow she was lying in the stranger's arms, both of them covered by a soft blanket. Her head was on his shoulder, her face buried in the curve where his neck met his shoulder.

He was asleep. She could tell by the deep, slow exhalations of his breath.

Move, she told herself. *Anna, for heaven's sake, shift away from him.*

Instead, she shifted closer. Closer. Drew his scent—masculine, musky, clean—deep into her lungs.

Her hand rose. By itself, surely. No way would she have deliberately lifted it, placed it against his jaw, rubbed her fingers lightly over the sexy stubble.

The sound of his breathing changed. Quickened. Her heartbeat quickened, too.

"Hello," he whispered.

Anna touched the tip of her tongue to her lips. "Hello," she whispered back.

His arms tightened around her. He turned his face, brought his lips against her palm in a soft kiss.

She heard a sound. Low, urgent…

The sound had come from her.

"I dreamed I was holding you," he said. His teeth fastened lightly in the tender flesh at the base of her thumb. "And then I awoke, and you were in my arms."

A tremor went through her. Or perhaps through him. She couldn't tell. And it didn't matter. The excitement growing within her was growing within him, too. His heartbeat had quickened. And when she shifted her weight, when she shifted her weight…

Yes. Oh, yes.

He was hard. Fully aroused. And she—dear God, she was, too. She could feel her breasts lift, her nipples bud. And she was wet. So wet…

He kissed her mouth. Her lips parted against

his. He groaned; his teeth fastened lightly in the tender flesh of her bottom lip, his tongue stroked across the tiny, exquisite wound and Anna gave a soft, pleading cry.

He murmured something in Italian. She didn't understand the words but she'd have had to be a fool not to understand their meaning.

His fingers tangled in her hair. Drew her head back. She could barely see his face in the dim light, but what she could see thrilled her—those dark eyes, the bones etched hard and harsh beneath his skin.

"You are playing with fire, *cara*," he said thickly.

Anna cupped her hand around the back of his head. "I like fire," she whispered.

"So do I." His voice was low, rough, as hot as his skin.

She brought his head down to hers, brushed her lips over his.

"I wanted you long before this," he said. "I wanted you hours ago, back in that lounge."

Anna trembled. Ran her fingers into his hair. It had been the same for her. That was why she'd argued with him. Fought with him. Because she had wanted him. Wanted this. His heat. His embrace. His strength…

She cried out as his hand slipped under her suit jacket. Under her blouse. Found her breast, cupped it over her silky bra, and she would have cried out again but he captured her lips with his, shaped her lips with his, slipped his tongue inside her mouth and claimed her with a slow, deep, kiss.

His thumb swept over her nipple.

She gasped, arched against him, felt her nipple bead and press blindly against his hand.

Please, Anna thought, *please…*

Draco gave a low growl.

He shifted the woman against him, raised her leg, brought it over his hip and pressed his aroused flesh against her.

Now, he thought, now…

The cabin lights winked on.

"Ladies and gentlemen, we'll be serving breakfast in just a few minutes…."

The woman in his arms froze. Her eyes flew open, blurred with passion and then with shock.

Cristo, he was having difficulty grasping the

facts himself. What had happened—what had *almost* happened…

Impossible.

He'd had sex on planes before. That was one of the perks of owning a private jet, but sex, or the closest thing to it, in a plane filled with people?

It was crazy.

How could he have done such a thing? It was an unacceptable, inexplicable loss of control, and he was not a man given to losses of control or, for that matter, to doing things that were either inexplicable or unacceptable.

"Let go of me," the woman snapped.

Draco looked at her. She was as white as paper, and trembling.

"Easy," he started to say, but she cut him short.

"Are you deaf? Let go!"

"Look, *bella,* I know you're upset—"

"Damnit, let go!"

His mouth thinned. Was she going to try to label him the villain in this little drama?

"With pleasure, once I'm convinced you're in control of your senses." He waited, watched her face. "Are you?"

"You'd better believe I am."

There was no panic in her voice now, only razor-sharp warning. A muscle knotted in Draco's jaw. Then, with elaborate care, he took his hands from her.

In a flash she tossed off the blanket, pushed the button that brought her seat upright, shot to her feet. He did the same, if a split second later.

"Listen to me," he said…

Too late.

She had already turned and fled.

CHAPTER FOUR

DRACO exited Fiumicino Airport, his cell phone at his ear.

"Just tell your boss that I am not, repeat, *not* going to meet his representative an hour from now. Two hours from now. That's the best I'll do. You don't know if you can get in touch with his rep?" Draco took the phone from his ear and glared at it. "That is not my problem—it is yours."

One good thing about old-fashioned desk phones, he thought grimly as he ended the call. In moments like this, you could slam the thing down and get some satisfaction out of it.

"Il mio principe!"

Heads swiveled. Glowering, Draco eyeballed his Maserati and his driver and strode toward them.

The man beamed. *"Buon giorno, il mio principe. Come è stato il vostro volo?"*

"My flight was a nightmare," Draco snarled, "and must you announce my title to the world?"

Merda. The driver's face fell. The man had been with him only a couple of weeks; he was just trying to be pleasant.

Draco took a deep breath, forced a smile he hoped was not a grimace to his lips.

"*Mi dispiace.* I'm sorry. I'm just jet-lagged."

"You must not apologize to me, sir! It is my fault, surely."

The driver clapped his heels together, lifted Draco's carry-on, and reached for the handle of the rear door just as Draco did the same. Their hands and arms collided.

Cristo! Could the man's face get any longer?

"*Scusi,*" the driver said in tones of hushed horror, "*Dio, signore, scusi...*"

"Benno. That is your name, is it not?"

"*Sì.* It is, sir, and I offer my deepest—"

"No. No apologies." Draco smiled again. At least, he pulled his lips back from his teeth. "Suppose we start over. You say 'Hello, how was your flight?' And I'll say—"

"*Scusi?*"

"I'll say," Draco said quickly, "it was fine. How's that?"

His driver looked bewildered. "As you wish, sir."

"Excellent," Draco replied, and he got into the backseat of the Maserati and sank into its leather embrace.

He was going to have to be careful.

He had put off the impending meeting with the Sicilian's man. That would, at least, give him time to shower, change his clothes, make some small attempt at getting his head on straight, but he was tired, not just jet-lagged but jet-fatigued.

Only that could explain what had happened on the plane.

"*Il mio principe?* Do you wish to go to your office or to your home?"

"Home, *per favore,* as quickly as possible, *sì?*"

"*Sì, il mio principe.*"

Draco sat back as the Maserati eased from the curb.

How could jet fatigue possibly be the reason for the incident on the plane? And what a hell of a way to describe that thing with the woman. What was that all about?

Draco frowned.

Well, he knew what it was all about.

He'd made love to her. And she'd made love to him, until those cursed lights went on, though he couldn't call what they'd been doing "making love."

It had been sex.

Mind-blowing, incredible sex.

Those few moments had been as exciting as any he'd ever spent with a woman.

He'd forgotten everything. Their surroundings, the fact that there were other people only a few feet away. All he'd known was her. Her taste. Her scent. Her heat.

There was a logical explanation, of course. There always was. For everything. In this case, the rush had come from having sex with a beautiful stranger in a place where anyone might have stumbled across them.

She'd been as out of control as he.

And then the lights had come on and she'd tried to lay it all on him.

No way, Draco thought, folding his arms over his chest.

All he'd done was watch her fall asleep, then

drawn the blanket over her. All right. It had been his blanket, not hers, but her blanket had been half-tucked under her.

It had been logical to use his.

How was he to know she would sigh and fling her arm across his chest? That she'd lay her head on his shoulder? He was a man, not a machine; she'd all but moved into his embrace. Was he supposed to push her away? And when she'd lifted her dark lashes and looked up at him, her eyes as blue as the sea, when she'd caressed his cheek...

Everything after that had been unplanned. Unstoppable. The kiss. The way she'd opened her mouth to his. The way she'd moaned when he cupped her breast, the way her heart had raced when he put his hand under her blouse...

Damnit, he was hard, just remembering.

Enough.

He'd made a mistake, and the sole value of a mistake was learning not to make it again.

No danger of that, he thought grimly. He would never see the woman again.

Besides, it was time to turn his mind elsewhere, to the meeting that would take place in just a couple of hours with the sleazy representative of a sleazy hoodlum. An hour wasted was what it would be, but at least he'd have the satisfaction of knowing he'd sent the Orsini stooge home to the States with his tail between his legs.

His phone rang.

Draco took it from his pocket. *"Pronto,"* he said brusquely. He listened, listened some more and then he snarled a word princes surely did not use and jammed the phone back into his pocket.

His attorney couldn't make the meeting. "Forgive me, sir," the man had said. "Reschedule it for whenever you like…"

Draco scowled.

The hell he would.

He had not flown all this distance to reschedule a meeting. It would go on as planned.

The day he couldn't handle a Sicilian's errand boy had not yet dawned.

His home was a villa in the parkland that surrounded the Via Appia Antica, ocher in color in keeping with its ancient Roman roots, set far back from the road and protected by massive iron gates.

He'd been drawn to the place the first time he

saw it, though what the draw had been was anybody's guess. The villa had been a disaster, part of it in total disrepair, the rest of it in desperate need of work.

Still, something about it had appealed to him. The history, he'd thought, the realization of what the house must have seen over the centuries.

Foolish, of course; a man with demanding responsibilities did not give in to sentimental drivel. He'd taken an acquaintance to see it. An architect. His report was not encouraging.

Draco, he'd said, *you want to do this, we'll do it. But the place is an ugly pile of rubble. Why spend millions on it when you already own a magnificent palazzo on the Tiber?*

It was an amazingly honest assessment. Draco told himself the man was right. Why not rebuild the Valenti palace? Once, a long time ago, he had promised himself that he would. His ancestors, his father, even his mother had stripped it of almost everything that could bring in cash and then neglected it to a state of near collapse, but he had the money to change all that.

So he had done it. Restored the palazzo to medieval grandeur. Everyone had pronounced it exquisite. Draco's choice of adjectives was far less flattering, though he kept his thoughts to himself.

You could breathe new life into a building, but you could not rewrite the memories it held.

He had gone back to the realtor who'd shown him the villa. He bought it that same day, restored it and moved in. There was an honesty to its rooms and gardens. Best of all, its ghosts wore togas.

The memories the villa held had nothing to do with him.

The Maserati came to a purring stop at the top of the driveway. The driver sprang from behind the wheel, but Draco was already out of the car and striding up the curved marble steps that led to the villa's massive wooden doors, which opened before he could touch them.

"Buon giorno, signore," his smiling house-keeper said, welcoming him home. Did he want something to eat? Breakfast? Some fruit and cheese, perhaps?

Coffee, Draco said. Not morning coffee. Espresso. A large pot, *per favore,* and he would have it in the sitting room in the master suite.

His rooms were warm; he suspected the windows had not been opened since he'd left for his San Francisco office three weeks ago. Now he flung them open, toed off his mocs, stripped off shirt, jeans, all his clothes, left them as part of a long trail that led to his bathroom.

He could hardly wait to shower away the endless hours of travel.

One of the first things he'd seen to when he'd arranged for the restoration of the villa was the master bath. He wanted a deep marble Jacuzzi, marble vanities and the room's centerpiece: a huge, glass-enclosed steam shower with multiple sprays.

His architect had raised an eyebrow. Draco had grinned. Life in America, he'd said, with all those oversize bathrooms, had spoiled him.

Perhaps it had.

His California duplex had a huge bathroom with a shower stall the size of a small bedroom. There were times, at the end of a long day, that he stood inside that stall and could almost feel the downpouring water easing the tension from him.

Now, standing in the shower at Villa Appia, Draco waited for that to happen.

Instead, an image suddenly filled his mind.

The blonde, here with him. Her hair undone, streaming like sunlight over her creamy shoulders, over her breasts, the pale apricot nipples uptilted, awaiting him.

He imagined his lips closed on those silken pearls, drawing them deep into his mouth.

His hand between her thighs.

Her hand on his erection.

Draco groaned.

He would back her against the glass, lift her in his arms, take her mouth as he brought her down, down, down on his hard, eager length….

Another groan, more guttural than the first, burst from his throat. His body shuddered, did what it had not done since he'd had his first woman at the age of seventeen.

Her fault, he thought in sudden fury. The blonde. She had made a fool of him yet another time.

He wished he could see her again, and make her pay.

Draco shut his eyes. Raised his face to the spray. Let the water wash everything from his body and his mind. He had to be alert for the meeting that loomed ahead.

The land in Sicily was his. He'd been in Palermo on business, gone for a drive to relax and passed through the town of Taormina, where something had drawn him to a narrow road, a hairpin curve, a heart-quickening view of the sea...

And a stretch of land that seemed unaccountably familiar.

He had taken the necessary steps to ensure his possession of it, brought in an architect... And suddenly received a letter from a man he'd never heard of, Cesare Orsini, who had made claims that were not only nonsense, they were lies.

The land was his. And it would remain his, despite the best efforts of a thug to claim it.

Draco had learned a very long time ago never to give in to bullies.

It was a lesson that had changed his life, one he would never, ever forget.

Anna's hotel was old.

Under some circumstances, that would have

been fine. After all, Rome was old. And magnificent.

The same could not be said about her hotel.

She'd made the reservation herself, online at something called BidCheap.com. Bidding cheap was where it was at; if only she'd had the common sense to demand her father hand over a credit card…

Never mind.

She'd traveled on the cheap before, after university and during spring breaks in law school. How bad could a place be?

Bad, she thought as she followed a shriveled bellman into a room the size of a postage stamp.

Water stains on the ceiling, heaven only knew what kinds of stains on the carpet, a sagging club chair in front of a window with a rousing view of…

An airshaft.

All the way to Rome so she could overlook an airshaft.

Well, so what?

She wouldn't be here long enough for it to matter. Besides, right now she felt as if she were walking in her sleep. She'd done that a couple of times, when she was little. Once she'd awakened in the kitchen, standing in front of the open fridge.

The next time, she'd been halfway out the conservatory door into the garden when she'd walked into one of her brothers. Falco, or maybe Rafe. Whichever, he'd startled her into wakefulness; she'd shocked him into a muffled oath.

"What are you—" they'd both said, and then they'd shushed each other and laughed, and agreed to keep quiet about the whole thing, because he'd obviously been sneaking back into the sleeping house and she'd just as obviously been sneaking out of it.

Anyway, she still remembered the feeling when her eyes had blinked open. She'd been awake, but not really. Her feet had seemed to be inches off the floor, her eyes had felt gritty, her body had felt...the only word that described it was *floaty*.

That was exactly how she felt now as she waited patiently for the bellman to finish showing her how to adjust the thermostat, how to open and close the drapes, how to use the minibar.

She yawned. Maybe he'd take the hint.

No way.

Now he was at the desk, opening drawers, snapping them shut, moving to the TV, turning it on and off, and, oh my God, now he was showing her how to set the clock radio...

Anna gave herself a mental slap on the forehead. Duh. He was waiting for a tip.

She opened her purse, dug inside, took out a couple of euros and, less than graciously, shoved them at him.

"Thank you," she said. "*Grazie*. You've been very helpful."

Her form would probably have earned demerits from Sister Margaret, who'd taught tenth grade deportment, but it satisfied the bellman, who smiled broadly, wished her a good day and exited, stage left.

"Thank God," Anna said, and fell facedown on the bed.

Everything ached.

Her arms from keeping her elbows tucked to her sides the last couple of hours of the flight. Her shoulders from hunching them. Her butt from pretty much doing the same kind of thing to keep her thighs and hips from coming into contact with Hannibal and the Hummer.

Her head hurt, too. A baby a couple of rows back had decided to scream in protest at the unfairness of life. Anna couldn't blame the kid; she'd have screamed, too, if it would have done any good.

But it wouldn't.

She had done something awful, and being packed into the middle seat would never be sufficient to expiate her total, complete, hideous feelings of embarrassment.

Anna groaned.

Embarrassment didn't even come close. Humiliation was an improvement, but horror was better. Much better. She was totally, completely, mind-numbingly horrified at what she'd done. What she'd almost done.

Okay, what she had done and what she had been on the way to doing...

His fault. The stranger's. All of it, his fault.

First, driving her temper into the stratosphere, then confusing her, then charming her.

An overstatement.

He had not charmed her. He could never be the charming type. He'd simply lulled her into thinking he was human. And maybe just a little bit interesting.

Pleasant conversation. A couple of smiles. His looks had been part of it, too. She had to admit, he was nice-looking.

A hunk, was more like it.

And then to wake up and find him all over her…

Anna sprang to her feet. Unzipped her carry-on.

"The bastard," she hissed as she tore through the contents in search of toothpaste, toothbrush, cosmetics.

Who gave a damn about his looks? He'd pawed her. Attacked her.

She groaned again and sank onto the edge of the bed.

"Liar," she whispered.

She was blaming everything on him when the truth was, whatever he had done, she had encouraged.

"How could you?" she whispered. "My God, Anna, how *could* you?"

The question was pointless. She didn't have an answer. And she was not a child.

You opened your mouth to a man's kisses, you moaned under his touch, you draped your leg over him... What could you call all that, if not encouragement?

The stranger hadn't done anything she hadn't wanted him to do.

Anna closed her eyes.

And, oh my, he had done it magnificently.

That wonderful, knowing mouth. That hard, long body. Those big hands on her breasts...

"Enough," she said briskly, and got to her feet.

She had things to do before the meeting. And, thankfully, miraculously, an hour in which to do them. Her father's *capo* had called on her cell. The prince had delayed the meeting by an hour.

Excellent news.

Not that she'd let the prince know it, Anna thought as she dumped the contents of her carry-on on the bed. On the contrary. She'd tell him that his change of plans—his unilaterally made change of plans—was an inconvenience. She would tell him of her flight, of how she had spent the entire time in the air diligently bent over her computer, studying the documents that proved, irrefutably, her mother's ownership of the land in—in whatever the name of that town in Sicily was. Torminia. Tarminia. Taormina, and she had less than an hour to at least get that much into her weary brain.

A shower. A change of clothes. A quick look at the file that had, thus far, proven useless.

Yes, but she'd gone into court with less information before and come out the winner.

She was one hell of a fine attorney.

The prince's attorney would probably be top grade, but so what? She could handle that. And she could definitely handle a fawned-upon, effeminate blue blood of a prince.

She was an American, after all.

Quickly she laid out fresh clothes. Another suit. Charcoal-gray, this time. Another blouse. Ivory silk, of course. A change of shoes. Stilettos. Black and glossy, with—for kicks—peep toes. Underwear. Silk. Sexy.

People could see the stilettos. The undies were just for her. She liked knowing that under the uniform she was all female.

The stranger would probably have liked it, too.

He was the kind of man who'd know how to strip a woman of a sexy half bra, a sexy thong.

There were times she'd thought, fleetingly, that what she'd worn under her clothes had been wasted on a lover.

It would not be wasted on him.

His hands would be sure and exciting as he took off her bra, his fingers just brushing across her nipples. They'd be steady as he hooked his thumbs into the edges of her thong and slid it down her hips, his eyes never leaving hers even as her breathing quickened, as she felt herself getting wet and hot and…and…

"Damnit!" she said. What was with her today?

She liked men. Liked sex. But this, wanting a man whose name she didn't even know, a man she'd never see again, not only wanting him but going into his arms in a place where anyone could have seen them…

Anna yanked her cell phone from her purse, hit a speed-dial digit. Her sister answered on the first ring.

"Anna?"

Oh, the wonders of caller ID.

"Izzy. I have something to ask you."

"Anna, where are you? I called your office and your secretary said—"

"Isabella," Anna said briskly, "how many times must I remind you? There are no more secretaries. She's a PA. A personal assistant. Got it?"

"Got it—but where are you? Your sec—your PA said you were in Italy, and I said that wasn't possible because you never told me that—"

"I'm in Italy, Iz. I never told you because I never had the chance. The old man cornered me Sunday—which, by the way, he could not have done if you'd shown up for dinner the way you were supposed to."

"I wasn't. I mean, nobody asked me to show up. And what's that got to do with you being in—"

"Later," Anna said impatiently. "Right now, just answer a question, okay?"

"What's the question?"

"It's…it's…" Anna cleared her throat. "You took psych, right?"

"Huh?"

"Izzy, I said—"

"I heard you. Sure. I took psych 101. So did you."

"Yeah. Well, remember that section on, ah, on sexual fantasies?"

"Anna," Isabella said carefully, "what's going on?"

"Wasn't there something about, ah, about fantasizing sex with a stranger?"

"A dark, dangerous stranger."

Anna put her fingers to her forehead, gave her temple a little rub.

"Right. And—and wasn't there something else about sex in public places? Where there was a risk of being caught?"

"Anna," Izzy said firmly, "what's going on?"

"Nothing. Nothing, I swear. I just—I just wanted to clarify something, is all."

"About risk? About sex with dangerous strangers? In public places? Hey, big sister, this is me, remember? What have you done?"

"I told you, nothing. I, ah, I read a magazine article on the plane. It was about sex. Risky sex. Hey, it's jet lag, you know? Makes you think strange things."

"Think them," Izzy said firmly. "Don't do them. I mean, you're not contemplating sex in a public place with a dangerous stranger, are you?"

Isabella lightened her question with a laugh. After a second, Anna laughed, too.

"Not even I would do something so crazy," she said, and then she said she had to run, that she'd phone when she had more time, kiss-kiss, talk to you soon...

And ended the call.

Silly to have called Isabella. The truth was, she'd intended to ask her if she'd ever wanted hot, fast sex with a stranger, and what would sweet Izzy know about sex, hot or otherwise?

Anna sighed. Undressed. Headed into the ancient bathroom, stepped into a rust-stained tub, tried not to bang her skull on the showerhead and turned a squeaking handle that wheezed out a thin stream of lukewarm water.

Forget the plane. The unintelligible files. Most of all, forget the man and what had happened. Correction. What had *almost* happened, because, thank goodness, she'd come to her senses in time.

What she had to concentrate on was the forthcoming meeting. The farcical concept of a prince in this, the twenty-first century. On making it crystal clear that no one, not even a doddering old stooge with a pretend crown on his balding pate and, for all she knew, a roomful of lawyers, could steal her mother's land and get away with it.

It was a good plan.

An excellent one.

It might have taken Anna far had she not, seventy-five minutes later, rushed through the doors of an elegant building just off the Via Condotti and paused at a reception desk only long enough to tell a receptionist elegant enough to grace the elegant building that she had an appointment with Prince Draco Valenti.

"And you are...?" the receptionist said, peering at Anna down her—what else could it have been?—Roman nose.

"I," Anna said, knowing it was time to marshal her resources, "I am counsel for Signore Cesare Orsini."

The receptionist nodded and reached for a telephone.

"Fourth floor, take a right, end of the corridor."

The elevator was elegant, too.

So was the man waiting for her. One man, not the legal team she'd anticipated. One man, standing at a window overlooking the street, his back to her.

Even so, he gave an immediate impression of... what?

Power, she thought. Power and strength, masculinity and youth. The tall, leanly muscled body evident within the stylish gray Armani suit; the broad shoulders; the long legs. He stood with those legs slightly apart; she could tell his arms were folded. His posture signaled irritation and arrogance.

Strange. There was something familiar about him...

Anna's heart leaped into her throat. *No,* she thought, *no!*

She made a sound, something between a choked gasp and a low moan. The man heard it.

"I do not appreciate being kept waiting," he said coldly as he swung toward her...

"You," Draco Valenti, *il Principe* Draco Marcellus Valenti of Rome and Sicily said, and the only good thing about this awful, terrible moment was that Anna knew the surprise and shock on his cold, classically beautiful face had to mirror hers.

CHAPTER FIVE

DRACO stared at the figure in the doorway.

No. No! It was not possible!

Lots of women had golden hair. Eyes the color of the Tyrrhenian Sea. A soft-looking, tender-pink mouth…

Dio, who was he trying to fool?

It was she. It was her. And what the hell did the intricacies of English grammar matter right now? He hadn't worried about his command of English in years, not since he'd taken the small financial company he'd started on equal parts bluff, brains and balls and turned it into an empire.

That a woman—that *this* woman—should turn his life so upside down proved that his brain was scrambled…

And, yes, impossible or not, it was the same woman. No question, no doubt. The unforget-table face, the curvaceous body demurely hidden within a dressed-for-success suit, the long legs set off by nothing-demure-about-them stiletto heels...

This was the woman he'd almost initiated into the Mile High club. Although *initiated* might be the wrong word. The way she'd come awake in his arms, the way she'd responded to his kisses...

For all he knew, she was a charter member.

Or wasn't.

She'd gone from hot to cold in the blink of an eye, and—

And who cared about that?

What was she doing here? She could be in Rome, yes. But she most assuredly could not be Cesare Orsini's representative.

Had she come looking for him? Maybe she hadn't been able to forget what had happened and now she wanted to finish that long, exciting slide into sexual oblivion...

Forget that.

His receptionist had buzzed him. *Cesare Orsini's representative is here, sir,* she'd said. And his receptionist had been with him a long time. No one could get past her without proper ID. So this had to be—it had to be—

The woman stopped in the doorway, face white.

"Ohmygod," she said. "Ohmygod!"

Draco's last, faint hope that this was a mistake vanished.

"You?" The woman reached for the doorjamb, curved her hand around it as if that might keep her from fainting. Her voice rose an octave. "You're Draco Valenti?"

Draco took a deep breath. "And you are…?"

She laughed, but it was not a real laugh. It was the kind of sound someone might make when what was really called for was an anguished wail of despair.

"The Orsini attorney."

Draco had always heard that hope died hard. Now he discovered that it didn't simply die—it crashed to earth in flames.

"Small world," he said drily.

She nodded. "Small, indeed." All at once the look of shock vanished. "Wait a minute," she said slowly, letting go of the jamb, straightening to her full height. Her eyes narrowed. "It was all deliberate!"

"I beg your pardon?"

Color suffused her face. "I cannot believe anyone would resort to such a thing."

"Perhaps you'd like to enlighten me, Miss—Miss—"

She stalked toward him menacingly, a cat approaching its prey.

"You set me up!"

"What?"

"You—you sneaky, slimy—"

"Watch what you say to me," Draco said sharply.

"You played me for a patsy!"

What did that mean? This woman was playing havoc in his head.

"You tried to take advantage of me!"

Draco gave a mirthless laugh.

"Are we back to that?" Slowly he let his gaze travel over her, from head to toe and back again. "Believe me, if I could erase that momentary behavioral aberration, I would."

A momentary behavioral aberration? Was that what he called what had happened—what had almost happened? And that chill in his eyes. In his voice. How could he speak so—so clinically of what had taken place on the plane?

Anna narrowed her eyes until they were slits.

"That behavioral aberration," she said, somehow making the words sound as if they consisted of four letters each, "was a clever ploy. At least, that's what you intended it to be. But it didn't work, did it? It didn't work because I'm not one of your—your women."

Draco raised an eyebrow. Looked over his shoulder. Stared into the corners of the elegant room.

"My women?" he purred.

She tossed her head.

"You know damned well what I mean. A man like you thinks he can snap his fingers and the entire female population of the planet will fall at his feet!"

"An interesting abuse of the laws of physics," he said coldly. "And what has it to do with you and me and that airplane?"

"You thought you could compromise my position."

"Was that the position you took when your leg was draped over mine?" Draco said with chilling politeness.

Her face turned an angry shade of crimson.

"You're despicable!"

"And you are wasting my time."

"You knew who I was all the time, Valenti!"

"You will address me as 'prince' or 'sir,'" Draco heard himself say, and tried not to wince at the idiocy of it, but what better way to deal with the representative of a smarmy Sicilian gangster than to play on the ancient, if ridiculous, elements of class distinction?

"That's why you invited me to sit with you."

"I hope you know what you're talking about, madam, because I most assuredly do not!"

She strode forward, came to a stop inches from him. The scent of her rose to him, something as feminine, delicate and sexy as her stiletto heels.

He recalled the scent from those moments she'd lain in his arms on the plane.

He recalled more than that.

The feel of her, pressed against him. The softness of her breasts against his chest. The heat of her body. The swift race of her heart against his, the sigh of her breath…

Draco frowned.

His body was remembering, too. Damnit, that was the wrong thing to have happen right now.

"You offered me that seat for a reason!"

"I offered it out of the goodness of my heart and the graciousness of my soul."

"Ha!"

She tossed her head again. A couple of golden curls slipped free of whatever it was women called those silly things they used to catch their hair and keep it from falling free, as nature had intended.

"How pathetic! That you'd stoop to such measures."

Her mouth was curled with contempt. Yes, he thought, but he could uncurl it in a heartbeat, kiss that mouth until it softened and sweetened under his.

"You—knew—who—I—was," she said hotly, punctuating the words by jabbing her index finger into the center of his chest. "And don't bother trying to deny it!"

Had he missed something? Had he been so busy remembering the taste of her, the feel of her, that he'd lost track of the conversation?

The realization made him even angrier.

"Deny what?" he demanded. "And stop doing

that," he growled, clasping her hand and folding his fingers around hers.

"What happened on the plane. What you did."

"Excuse me?"

"Kissing me. It was all for a purpose."

He laughed. He couldn't help it. What man wouldn't laugh at such an accusation?

Her eyes flashed with anger. "You think this is amusing?"

"Let me be sure I understand this. You're accusing me of kissing you on purpose?"

"Absolutely."

"Well, that's a relief. I mean, I'd hate to have you accuse me of kissing you without any purpose."

Anna blinked. How could he do this? Twist her words so they came out wrong. Take her accusations and turn them into jokes.

Most of all, how could he be so damnably arrogant and officious and clever and still be so incredibly easy on the eyes? How could the feel of his fingers wrapped around her wrist make her remember the feel of his body against hers? The feel of his mouth? The taste of his kisses?

"Don't play dumb," she said. "You thought if

you seduced me it would be impossible for me to represent Cesare Orsini's interests."

He gave her a long, steady look. Then, curse the man, he laughed. Again.

"*Dio,* am I clever!"

"What you are is a bast——"

"I hate to rewrite your script, madam, but you've got it all wrong. I had no idea who you were. The only thing I knew about you was that you had one hell of a quick temper."

"What I have, oh your worshipful highness, is no tolerance for bull."

"A quick temper. A sharp tongue." Suddenly his voice turned low and rough. "And you fell asleep in my arms and came awake wanting me as much as I wanted you."

Anna's heart banged against her ribs.

"I was half-asleep. You took advantage. You wanted to compromise me."

He gave a soft, sexy laugh.

"*Compromise* is not the word to describe what I wanted of you." His arms went around her. "What we wanted of each other."

"Let go," Anna said.

"That's what you said on the plane."

"Exactly. And I'm saying it again. Let—"

"You said it only after the lights came on." His arms tightened around her; she could feel every inch of him against her. "Until then, you were as turned on as I was."

"That isn't true! I wasn't—"

His gaze dropped to her lips. She could almost feel the warmth of his mouth on hers, taste those remembered kisses.

"The hell you weren't."

His voice was husky. Hot with masculine warning. He was aroused. The hard ridge of his erection was against her belly.

Desire, urgent and primitive, shot through her blood. He was the enemy. He was everything she despised, a damnable aristocrat, a man who obviously thought he could treat a woman as if he owned her. He was her father's and her mother's enemy, for heaven's sake...

But what did that matter when her body throbbed with need?

They could finish what had started hours ago.

Alone. Here, with no prying eyes to see them, no one to interrupt a joining of eager bodies.

Anna shuddered. A whisper of sound sighed

from her mouth. Her lashes fell, veiled her eyes as she rose toward him…

His arms opened, dropped to his sides.

She blinked. Looked up. Saw that his face was stony, his mouth cruel.

"Now," he said calmly as he took a step back, "now, *signorina,* you have been compromised."

Her hand balled into a fist at her side. She wanted to hit him. Hard. Leave an imprint on that smug, cold, handsome face.

"You did that once," he said coldly. "I would advise you not to do it again."

Anna took a steadying breath. And laughed, though it took everything she possessed to choke out the sound.

"You're so easy, Your Highness. Oh, sorry. Does the news come as a shock? Do you honestly believe one look from you turns my knees to water?"

Draco narrowed his gaze.

What he believed was that she was lying. To him. To herself. If he wanted her, he could have her. Now. Here. But he didn't. Damnit, he didn't. What he wanted was to get everything to do with Cesare Orsini out of his life.

"Enough of these games," he growled. "What is your name? And what do you want?"

"I want you to face facts." Anna's voice was steady. Amazing, because her pulse was ragged. "No matter what you claim, I can make an excellent case for you knowing my identity all along." She smiled brightly. "So if you want to talk about compromising one's legal position…"

"An excellent speech. Unfortunately, it's also meaningless. I didn't know your name on that plane. I still don't."

Anna gave a negligent shrug. "He said, she said. Stuff like that is bread and butter in courts of law."

"Which brings me to the second reason your little speech is meaningless." He smiled. "This would never get adjudicated in a court of law."

"I'm an attorney."

Another quick smile, this one pure venom. "Not in Italy."

Damnit, he was quick, and he was right. She had no legal standing here. She'd tried telling that to her father. *You want a lawyer, find one who's Italian,* she'd said, but Cesare had been adamant. This was a family matter. A personal matter. He didn't need a stranger to speak for him, for Sofia. He needed her.

"So," the Prince of All He Surveyed said, "we have a—what would you call it? A situation. I am the rightful owner of land your client would like to claim is his."

"The land in question belongs to my client's wife. *She* is the rightful owner."

Draco shrugged, walked to his impressive desk, hitched a hip onto its edge.

"I agreed to meet with Cesare Orsini's representative as a courtesy."

"You agreed," Anna said coolly, "because you know you have a problem on your hands."

She wasn't wrong. There were those in the judiciary who would be more than happy to see a Valenti prince trapped in endless legal wrangling over a mess like this. The land was indisputably his, but thanks to the way things worked in Sicily, it could take years to put the case to rest.

Assuming there was a case, and there wouldn't be.

He knew enough about Cesare Orsini and men like him to understand they had only two methods of settling debts.

One involved blood.

The other...

Draco sighed. His plane was back in service; his pilot was already en route to Rome so he could fly him back to Hawaii, the sea, the sun and the warm bed of his mistress—a woman who would not play hot then cold, as this one did.

"Very well." He went behind the desk, sat down in a chair, pulled open a drawer, took out a gold pen and a leather checkbook. "How much?"

"I beg your pardon? How much what?"

"Didn't you hear what I said? I'm tired of playing games. How much does Orsini want?"

"To buy his land?"

A muscle knotted in Draco's jaw. "The land is not his to sell."

The woman gave him a smile that would have sent a diabetic to the hospital. She was going to drive him crazy!

"I am not offering to buy it, I am offering—"

"A payoff?"

"Compensation. What does your client want to end this insane charade?"

Anna tossed her briefcase on a chair and strolled to the enormous desk. It was probably very old, and obviously hand carved. Mythological griffins dove on falcons, falcons dove on rabbits, wolves sank their fangs into the hindquarters of stags and brought them to their knees.

The history of the landed gentry, she thought coldly. She knew a lot about that history. She'd made a point of studying it when she'd first realized her father's true profession, hoping against hope that understanding the old Sicilian antagonisms would help her understand him.

What she'd ended up understanding was that the world could be a brutally unfair place, but the world of her father was more than brutal.

Right now, though, what she was seeing firsthand went a long way toward validating her opinion of princes who thought they could take whatever they wanted from mere mortals, and get away with it.

"Well?"

She looked up. The prince, gold pen poised, was watching her much as the wolves carved into his desk had surely watched the creatures they hunted. He looked intent. Determined. Coldly analytical, and certain of how the chase would end.

Not so fast, big boy, she thought, and she took a long breath.

"Well, what?"

"You're pushing your luck," Draco said softly.

"And you're making foolish assumptions if you think you can buy your way out of this." Anna jerked her chin toward the checkbook. "You can put that thing away."

Draco said nothing for a long minute. A muscle knotted and unknotted in his jaw. Then he dropped the pen and checkbook back into the drawer and slammed it shut with enough force to send the sound bouncing around the room.

"Let's get down to basics," he snapped. "If you don't want money, what do you want?"

"You know what I want. The land, of course."

"That's impossible. The land is mine. I have the deed to it. No court in Sicily will—"

"Perhaps not."

"Then, how—"

Anna gave him her best look of wide-eyed innocence.

"Roman Aristocrat Steals Land from Helpless Grandmother," she said sweetly, and batted her

lashes. "Maybe they can work the words *puppies* and *kittens* into that headline, too."

"You left something out. *Sicilian Citizen Protects Land from Theft by American Hoodlum.*" Draco flashed a smug smile. "Or don't you like that wording?"

"You're no more Sicilian than I am!"

"My ancestors settled in Sicily five hundred years ago."

"You mean they invaded it five hundred years ago. The Orsinis were already there."

"I asked you a question. What do you want?"

"And I answered it. I want the land. If you think my client will run from a newspaper calling him a gangster..." Anna showed her teeth in a brilliant smile. "Trust me, Valenti. It won't be the first time."

"Do not address me that way," Draco said, hating himself for sounding ridiculous, hating the woman for pushing him to it. "As for headlines..." He shrugged. "They come and go."

She smiled. It was the kind of smile that made him want to shoot to his feet and toss her out of his office...

Or take her in his arms and remind her of just

how easily he could change her cold contempt to hot desire.

"The thing is, oh powerful prince, we love that kind of stuff in the States. We give it all our attention. Page Six of the *Post. People. US. The Star.* All those juicy tabloids, the even juicier internet blogs. The cable news channels."

"You're pushing your luck again," he said in a soft voice.

She knew she was, but it was too late to back down now.

"Even the real newspapers—the *New York Times,* the *San Francisco Chronicle,* the *Washington Post*—will love this." Anna leaned closer. "See, one of the few things I had time to do was look you up on Google. I know you're not just a prince, stealing money from the peasants—"

"A gangster's legal mouthpiece calling me a thief?" Draco leaned back in his chair, folded his arms over his chest and laughed.

"You also control a huge financial empire."

His laughter ended. A look of cold determination took its place as he rose to his feet

"If you have a point, get to it."

"Oh, I do," Anna said. She paused for effect, as if this were a grungy New York City courtroom instead of an elegant office. "How do you think a company like yours would stand up to such a scandal in today's financial climate?"

His face darkened.

"How dare you threaten me? Who the hell are you?"

Anna dug into her pocket, took out a small leather case and extracted a business card. Nonchalantly she plucked a pen from his desk, scribbled the name of her hotel on the back, then flipped the card at him. He caught it, read the black engraving and looked at her through narrowed eyes.

"Anna Orsini," he said softly. "Well, well, well."

"That's me," Anna said cheerfully. "Anna Orsini. Cesare's daughter." Her voice became cold and flat. "In other words, a full-blooded member of the Orsini *famiglia*. I urge you to keep that in mind."

It seemed the right line, the closing line, especially when your enemy looked as if he might spring across the desk and throttle you...

Especially when your own heart was banging so hard you were afraid it might leap from your chest.

Anna pivoted on her heel, picked up her briefcase and walked out.

CHAPTER SIX

DRACO watched Anna Orsini march to the door.

Head up, shoulders back, spine straight, her long-legged stride on those amazing stilettos clearly sending a to-hell-with-you message.

Almost.

The shoes changed her walk, ever so slightly. Balancing on them made her hips sway, changing what she surely meant to be a brisk march into something feminine and damned near feline.

Golden-haired seductress. Cold-blooded *consigliere.* Which was the real Anna Orsini?

For a dangerous couple of seconds Draco came close to demanding the answer.

He would go after her, swing her toward him, look down into those blue eyes and say, *Hell, woman, how dare you threaten me! Are you fool enough to think I can be brought to heel by you and your hoodlum father?*

Or he'd say nothing at all.

He'd pull her into his arms, lower his head to hers and kiss her hard and deep until she forgot about being her father's mouthpiece and became the woman he'd known on the plane, the one who'd come within a heartbeat of giving herself up to him.

Instead, he stood his ground. He didn't even breathe until she slammed the door hard enough to make it rattle.

He had to move carefully. No rash decisions. No letting the emotions within him overtake logic.

Draco went to his desk and sat in the massive chair behind it.

No question, he had a problem. Anna's threat had teeth.

Teeth?

Hell, it had fangs, fangs that could sink into his throat and destroy him. There were some businesses that sought publicity, that thrived on it.

Not Valenti Investments.

Even being mentioned in the same breath as a crook like Cesare Orsini could mean the end of everything he had worked for. Not just money, although the amount he might lose, for himself and for his clients, was staggering.

But there was more at stake than money. If Anna forced a public confrontation, Draco would lose that which mattered most to him.

The honor of his name. The respect it once again carried.

A muscle jumped in his cheek.

To think he'd almost had sex with her. With Cesare Orsini's *consigliere.*

Cristo, he wanted to laugh!

Not that this was a laughing matter, Draco thought grimly as he took the gangster's letters from his briefcase and stacked them on the desk in front of him. Nothing about the situation was even remotely amusing.

If only he'd known who she was last night, he'd never have let things go so far.

Actually, the more he thought about it, the less he understood why he had become involved with her at all.

Her name could be Jane Doe, and he wouldn't want her.

She wasn't his type. She was too tall, too blonde,

too slender. His tastes ran to petite women. Bru-
nettes, with voluptuous bodies.

And that attitude of hers, that feminist chip she
carried on her shoulder...

What man in his right mind would be attracted
to a woman who argued over everything?

Calmer now, he could see that it had been the
situation, not the woman, that had turned him on.
The hushed darkness. The isolation that came of
being five miles above the earth. The added rush
of knowing you were in a public setting.

Draco sat back in his chair.

Given all that, what man would not want to take
things to their natural conclusion when he awoke
with a woman draped over him like a blanket?

In a way, he owed Anna Orsini his thanks. Men
thought with parts of their anatomy that had nothing to do with their brains. She had saved them
both from making an embarrassing mistake.

Imagine if he'd actually had sex with the Orsini
consigliere...

Draco did laugh this time.

There was a solution to the problem. There
always was. And he would find it—something

he could do to get the Orsinis, father and daughter, out of his life.

He was, above all else, a logical man. A pragmatist. And pragmatism, not emotion, would save the day. Control over your emotions was everything.

His father and those before him had never understood that.

They drank to excess. Gambled with money they didn't have. They went from woman to woman, losing themselves in the kind of passion and intensity that could only lead to trouble.

The Valenti family history was a minefield of greed, infidelity, abandonment and divorce.

Absolutely, a man had to learn to curb his emotions. And Draco had learned early how to curb his.

His boyhood had been filled with scenes that still made him grimace. His mother had taken a string of lovers who helped themselves to what little remained of the family's money. Still, she'd apparently found her life boring and abandoned her husband and Draco when he was a toddler.

His father might as well have done the same. He was too busy whoring and gambling to pay attention to his son. Draco's early memories were of big, silent rooms, most of them stripped of what had once been elegant furnishings. The few servants who remained, overworked and underpaid, ignored him.

He had been a solitary and lonely child; it had never occurred to him other children might have had different existences from his.

One winter, his father stayed sober long enough to figure out that the last of what he'd still referred to as his staff had abandoned ship, leaving nine-year-old Draco to fend for himself.

The prince had given his young son orders to bathe and dress in his best clothes. Then he'd taken him to a school run by nuns.

The Mother Superior, who was also the principal, had eyed Draco and wrinkled her nose, as if he gave off a bad smell. She'd tested him in math. In science. In French and English.

Draco had known the answers to all her questions. He was a bright boy. An omnivorous reader. From age five he'd sought solace by immersing himself in the few remaining volumes in the once-proud Valenti library.

But he'd been struck speechless.

The nun's voice had been sharp; he'd been able to see his own reflection in her eyeglasses, and that was somehow disorienting. Her coif had made her round face with its pointed nose look like an owl's.

She had been, in his eyes, an alien creature, and he'd been terrified.

"Answer the Mother Superior," his father had hissed.

Draco had opened his mouth, then shut it. The nun glared at his father, then at him.

"The boy is retarded," she'd said. Her fingers had clamped hard on Draco's shoulder. "Leave him with us, Prince Valenti. We will, if nothing else, teach him to fear his God."

That was the theology he'd received at the hands of the sisters.

The other boys had taught him more earthly things to fear.

Beatings, on what was supposed to be the playground. Beatings at night, in the sour-smelling dormitory rooms. Humiliation after humiliation.

It had been the equivalent of tossing a puppy into a cage of hungry wolves.

Draco had been skinny and pale. His clothes

were threadbare, but their style had marked him as a member of a despised upper class, as had the way in which he spoke. He was quiet, shy and bookish, with the formal manners of a boy who had never before dealt with other children.

It had been a recipe for disaster, either unnoticed or ignored by the sisters until one day, almost a year later, when Draco had decided he could not take any more.

It was lunchtime, and everyone had been on the playground. Draco saw one of his tormenters closing in.

All the hurt, the fear, the emotions he'd kept bottled inside him burst free.

He'd sprung at the other boy. The fight had turned ugly, but when it was over, the other kid was on the ground, sobbing. Draco, bloodied and bruised but victorious, had stood over him.

His reputation was made. And if keeping it meant stepping up to the challenge of other boys from time to time, beating them and, occasionally, being beaten in return, so be it.

The Mother Superior had said she'd always known he would come to no good.

The day he turned seventeen, one of the senior

boys decided to give him a very special gift. He'd come to Draco during the night while he slept, slapped a hand over his mouth and yanked down his pajama bottoms.

Draco was no longer small or skinny. He had grown into manhood; he was six foot three inches of fight-hardened muscle.

With a roar, he'd shot up in bed, grabbed his attacker by the throat and if the other boys hadn't pulled him off, he might have killed him.

The Mother Superior asked no questions.

"You are," she told Draco, "a monster. You will never amount to anything. And you are unwanted here."

He hadn't argued. As far as he knew, she was right on all counts.

She'd expelled him, told him to be gone the next morning, and he'd thought, *So be it.*

That night he'd jimmied the lock on the door to her office and taken four hundred euros from her desk. Going home was not an option. He had no home, not really. The castle was in a state of near disaster and his father, who had visited him once the first year and then never again, meant nothing to him.

The next day he'd flown to New York with the clothes on his back, a determination to make something of himself, and a philosophy by which to live.

Never show weakness.

Never show emotion.

Trust no one but yourself.

New York was big, brash and unforgiving. It was also a place where anything was possible. For Draco, that "anything" meant finding a way to make sure he'd seen the last of hunger, poverty and humiliation.

He'd found jobs. In construction. As a waiter. A cab driver. He'd worked his royal ass off—not that anybody knew he was a royal. And in the dark of night, in a roach-infested room in a part of Brooklyn that was beyond any hope of gentrification, he'd lie awake and admit to himself that he was going nowhere.

A man needed a goal. A purpose. He'd had neither.

Until, purely by accident, he'd learned that his father had died.

Prince Mario Valenti, a one-inch item buried

in the *New York Post* said, *died yesterday in a shooting accident involving former movie star...*

The details didn't matter. His father had died a shameful death, broke and in debt. And in that moment Draco had known what he would do with his life.

He would redeem the Valenti name.

That meant paying off his father's debts. Restoring the castle. Making the family name, even the accursedly ridiculous title, stand for something again.

He'd wanted a new start. To get it, he'd worked his way across the vast expanse of the United States. He liked Los Angeles, but San Francisco struck him as not just beautiful but the kind of place that rewarded individuality. He'd talked himself into San Francisco State University, chosen classes in mathematics and finance because he found them interesting. Writing a term paper, he'd stumbled upon an idea. An investment plan. It worked in theory but would it in real life?

Only one way to find out.

Draco took everything he'd set aside for the next year's tuition and sank it in the stock market.

His money doubled. Tripled. Quadrupled. He quit school, devoted himself to investing.

And parlayed what he had into a not-so-small fortune.

"Draco Valenti," the *Wall Street Journal* said the first time it mentioned him, "a new investor on the scene, who plays the market with icy skill."

Was there any other way to play the market or, in fact, to play the game of life?

Eventually he founded his own company. Valenti Investments. He made mistakes, but mostly he made choices that led to dazzling successes.

He knew the dot com ride would not last forever, and acted accordingly. He thought packaged mortgages sold by banks made no sense and he bet his money, instead, on their eventual failure. He found small tech firms with big ideas and invested in them.

He made more money than seemed humanly possible, enough to buy the San Francisco condo, the Roman villa. Enough to restore the Valenti castle.

And enough to fund a school for poor kids in Rome and others in Sicily, New York and San

Francisco, though he kept those endeavors strictly private.

He was tough, he was hard, he was not sentimental. The schools were simply a practical way of using up some of his money, and he'd be damned if he'd let anybody try to put a different spin on it.

Draco shoved aside the Orsini documents and swung his chair toward the window behind him.

There had to be a way around the Orsini problem.

Valenti Investments could not, must not, go under. He could live through the financial loss— hell, life was, at best, an uphill battle—but to tarnish the Valenti name...

He could not bear the thought of that happening again.

He turned from the window.

There was a solution, and he would find it, but not by concentrating on it. He would, instead, do what he always did at moments of stress. He would think about anything but the problem at hand. He would think logically. Rid his thoughts of emotion.

Draco rang the intercom. His PA answered.

"I have some letters to dictate," he said.

But, damnit, Anna Orsini would not stay in the mental file drawer in which he'd placed her. She kept appearing in his mind, front and center.

Ridiculous, because she was not really the problem. Her father was.

Then why did he keep seeing her face, that sleepy, sexy look in her eyes when she'd lain in his arms last night?

Why did he keep remembering the way she dressed, the conservative suit, the do-me stilettos?

What did she have on under that suit? Was it the equivalent of banker's gray? Or was it silk and lace, as sexy as the shoes?

"Sir?" his PA said.

Draco blinked.

"Sorry," he said briskly. "Uh, where was I?"

"The Tolland merger," his PA said, and Draco nodded and picked up where he'd left off in his dictation.

Five minutes later, he gave up.

"That's all for now, Sylvana," he said.

His PA left the room. Draco rose to his feet,

grabbed his suit coat and went to lunch. He followed that with a long, hard workout at his gym.

He still had not come up with a way to handle the Orsini situation.

Worse, Anna Orsini was still in his head.

At five, he called for his car.

"Where to, sir?" his driver said.

Draco thought of the various answers he could give.

He could go out to dinner. He had no reservations anywhere, but that would not matter. There was not a *ristorante* in Rome that would not give him its best table if he showed up at the door.

He could take out his BlackBerry, phone one of a dozen beautiful women. There wasn't one in Rome who would deny him anything he might ask of her, even at the last minute.

That made him think of his mistress, waiting for him in Hawaii.

Cristo, he had not thought of her once the entire day.

"Take me home," he told his driver, and while the big car made its way through the crushing end-of-day traffic, Draco put through a call to her.

"Hello?" she said in a sleepy voice.

What time was it in Hawaii, anyway? No way was he going to ask.

"It's me," he said. "How are you?"

"Draco," she said. He could picture the look on her face. Sultry, sexy, pouty. "I thought you'd forgotten me."

Draco rubbed his temple with his free hand.

"How did you spend your day?" he said, because he knew he had to say something.

She laughed.

"I spent it shopping, darling. Well, window-shopping. I have a whole bunch of gorgeous things picked out for you to buy me when you get back."

Draco closed his eyes and imagined the hours she'd expect him to spend in a dozen different boutiques.

"When *will* you be back, Draco?" Her voice turned husky. "I miss you."

The truth was she missed the status that came of being seen with him. The knowledge that he would buy her whatever she'd shopped for today. She missed his title, his status, his money.

And, yes, his looks, and his expertise in bed.

It would be foolish to deny that women liked both.

"Darling? When will you be back?"

He wouldn't be.

The realization was sudden, and so was its full meaning.

Draco cleared his throat.

"Something's come up," he said. "So, ah, so here's what I suggest. Stay on a few more days. Do some shopping—tell the shops to phone my office and they'll okay the charges. Take your time. Enjoy yourself. When we're both back on the coast, I'll give you a call."

Silence. Then she said, "And when, exactly, will that be?"

Her tone was cool. She was not a stupid woman, not when it came to men and the ways of the world. Their two-month relationship was over; Draco had not even realized it until this minute.

"I don't know," he said with brutal honesty. "But I do know that I wish you only the best."

He disconnected, put his BlackBerry in his pocket as the car pulled through the gates that led to his villa.

He had not planned on ending things just now. Soon, yes. But why now?

An image flashed into his mind.

Anna Orsini.

Naked this time, her golden hair loose on his pillows, her arms raised to him…

"Signore?"

The car had stopped at the foot of the steps to the villa. His driver stood beside the open rear door. Draco climbed out, told him he was free for the rest of the evening, went into the house and told his housekeeper the same thing.

She had left a salad for him. He ate it, had a cold beer and went to his rooms, where he undressed and stepped into the big steam shower.

Maybe the hot water would work the tension from his shoulders and neck.

Maybe it would wash away the image of Anna, naked, hot and silken under the stroke of his hand.

Draco cursed, stepped from the shower, wrapped a towel around his hips.

She had accused him of playing her, but he was the one being played!

An entire day wasted. And for what? He had

money. Power. He could take on the entire Orsini *famiglia* and break it.

Why had he been so civilized when she showed up at his office? He should have told her to get the hell out. Of his office, of his life, of Rome.

And that exit she'd made. Gloating. Egotistical. As if she were the royal and he was the commoner—and wasn't it pathetic she had him thinking such crap?

Anna Orsini needed to be put in her place. Reminded that she was a woman, not *consigliere* to a gangster.

And he could have reminded her. In the most basic way possible. Gone after her, slapped his hand on the door to keep her from opening it. Locked the damned thing, then finished what had begun somewhere high over the Atlantic, because that was what this was all about, not land, not her father, not anything but a man and a woman and frustrated desire.

He could see her in his mind's eye, stripped to her soft skin, that mass of golden hair unbound, drifting over her shoulders, over her breasts. He'd put his mouth to the pebbled tips, his hand between her thighs, his fingers searching out her hot, wet heat because she *would* be hot and wet, eager, *Dio,* hungry for him, only for him.

Draco's instant erection pushed hard against the towel draped around his hips. He said a word that came straight from the schoolyard of his childhood, but the urgency that accompanied it was solely that of a man.

Basta! Enough.

He had met Anna Orsini only last night, but she had already turned his life upside down. He could think about nothing but her.

And he had let her do this to him. He had permitted it.

Quickly, he tossed the towel aside, pulled on boxers, a pair of age-softened jeans, a black T-shirt, a pair of mocs.

His wallet, with her business card in it, was on a small table near the front door, where he'd left it. He yanked the card out and looked at it. He had never heard of her hotel, but he knew the location.

It would take him half an hour to get there.

He could have phoned her, but that wouldn't be half as satisfying as confronting her.

Do your worst, he'd say. *Go to the media.*

Spread whatever story you like, write it across the sky.

He would withstand the ugly publicity. Hell, he'd turn it in his favor. A hoodlum and his daughter, threatening Prince Draco Valenti?

Draco gave an ugly laugh.

He had money. Power. Far more of both than Cesare Orsini could ever hope to have. And he would use them both.

By the time he was done with the old man and his daughter, they would wish to God they'd never even heard of him.

There were three cars, and the keys to them, in his garage. The big Maserati limo, a red Lamborghini and a black Ferrari. He got behind the wheel of the Ferrari.

The car was fast and powerful and it suited the rage boiling within him.

He made the drive in fifteen minutes, his foot to the floor, cutting off whatever vehicle was in his way, ignoring the bleat of horns and raised fingers of the drivers he sped past.

The car's tires squealed as he brought it to a stop in the hotel's driveway. A uniformed doorman approached, hand raised, to tell him he couldn't park there. Draco tossed him a hundred-euro note and moved quickly through the front door.

The desk clerk looked up at his approach.

"May I help you," he started to say, but Draco cut him short.

"Anna Orsini. What room?"

"I am sorry, *signore,* but I cannot—"

Draco reached across the desk, grabbed the clerk by the tie and hauled him forward.

"What room?" he growled.

"Three—three fourteen," the clerk sputtered.

Draco nodded, dropped another hundred-euro note on the counter.

There were two elevators, one in use, one with an out-of-order sign taped to its door. He waited a couple of seconds for the one that was supposedly operating and then he took the stairs instead.

Room 314 was at the end of a dark hall. He strode along a frayed carpet runner until he reached it and then he hit the door once, with his fist.

It opened instantly.

"Wow," Anna said, "that's the quickest room service I ever—"

"Anna."

She was barefoot, swaddled in a voluminous white terry-cloth robe, her face bare of makeup and as beautiful as any ever sculpted by Michelangelo. Her hair was a damp tumble of golden curls; her eyes were wide with shock and as blue as the deepest part of the sea.

"Draco?" she whispered.

He stepped into the room. Shut the door behind him without once looking away from her.

"I am not room service," he said in a low voice. "And I am not a man you can toy with." He paused. He could feel the rage in him changing to something dark and hot and far more dangerous.

"Anna," he said roughly, "goddamnit, Anna…"

"Goddamnit, Draco," Anna said, "what took you so long?"

And then…

Then she was in his arms.

CHAPTER SEVEN

ANNA was on her toes, her body tight against Draco's, her arms wound around his neck.

His mouth was on hers, open, demanding and merciless. His hands were under her robe, hard and hot on her skin, cupping her bottom and lifting her into him. His erection pressed urgently against her belly, the masculine power surging against his closed fly, sent hot shudders of excitement racing through her.

She had had lovers before. Anticipating the moment, the first electric shimmer of desire, was always thrilling.

But never like this.

She was trembling, breathless, almost dizzy with need.

Draco said something, the words rushed and urgent. She couldn't understand them; he spoke in the kind of elegant, upper-class Italian that was nothing like the Sicilian dialect she'd heard as a child, but she didn't have to make sense of the words to know their meaning.

Draco wanted her.

Right now. Right here.

It was what she wanted, too.

He untied her robe, shoved it back on her shoulders. His hands swept over her, down her spine, kneading her hips, then rising up her torso to cup her breasts.

His thumbs moved over her nipples and a cry broke from her throat. Anna caught his black T-shirt in her fists and tugged it free of his jeans. She put her palms flat against his naked chest, and he groaned.

She answered his groan with one of her own.

The feel of his body!

His skin was hot, hair-roughened. He was all muscle, and when she ran her hands down his belly, to the jeans he wore low on his hips, her fingers marveled over the ridged, perfect abs.

"Draco," she whispered.

He growled her name, pushed her robe away and it fell to her feet. The air felt cool on her overheated flesh; he bent his head, kissed her throat, the slope of one breast, drew its beaded tip deep into his mouth.

Anna cried out; her head fell back and a curl of flame swept from low in her belly directly to where Draco's mouth worked its magic.

He raised his head, kissed her deeply, thrust his fingers into her hair and took her mouth again and again.

Now his hands were on her. All over her. His caresses were not gentle, but gentle wasn't what she wanted.

Not now.

What she wanted was this. Draco's lips at her throat. His fingers on her nipples. His denim-clad knee between her thighs.

And then his hand. Oh, his hand, cupping her. His fingers parting her.

"Hot," he said thickly. "So hot and wet…"

She sobbed his name, felt her body weeping with hunger against his palm.

"Oh God, hurry!" she said. "Oh, hurry!"

He made a sound deep in his throat as he unzipped his fly. Anna pushed his hand aside, reached for his straining flesh. Her heart pounded as his erection sprang free. Her breath hissed as she closed her fingers around the silk-over-steel power of his hardened flesh.

He was big. Incredibly big, and she gasped as she wrapped her hand around him.

"Anna," he said, only that, but the single word was so filled with urgency that she rose on her toes and nipped at his bottom lip.

"Yes," she said against his mouth, "please, please…"

It was the soft, desperate plea that was his final undoing.

Draco scooped her into his arms, swung around and pushed her back against the closed door. She wrapped her legs around his hips. He grunted and drove into her.

Her scream was everything a man could want, the cry of a woman swept away by passion.

He thrust into her again. And again. Harder and harder as she cried out in ecstasy.

"Draco," she sobbed, "oh, sweet heaven, Draco…"

He shifted her weight, one powerful arm around her buttocks, one angled against her back, his hand in her hair so that his mouth could plunder hers.

He was relentless. Kissing her. Thrusting into her. She was panting, sobbing, riding him and riding him and he was going to come, *Dio,* he was going to come….

Anna screamed.

And Draco exploded deep, deep inside her.

The world stood still.

After a very long time Anna drew a ragged breath. Her head fell forward onto Draco's shoulder, and she buried her face against his throat.

Her heart felt as if it were trying to pound its way out of her chest, or was that racing beat his?

She sighed and closed her eyes.

He held her tight, and she all but purred.

"Wow," she said in a shaky whisper. "That was— it was…"

Draco laughed softly. "*Sì.* It certainly was." He hesitated. "It was not too quick?"

Anna lifted her head.

"You just want to hear me say 'wow' again."

He grinned. "Perhaps. But I was too fast."

"No. You weren't. And if you keep apologizing, I won't let you do this again." Her lips curved in a wickedly sexy smile. "At least, I won't let you do it more than another two or three dozen times."

Laughter rumbled in his chest.

"Is that all?" he teased, and he swung her into his arms, carried her to the bed, tumbled onto it with her. "Sorry, Orsini. Twenty or thirty times isn't going to be enough."

Anna looped her arms around his neck.

"You're right," she said softly. "It won't be."

Draco kissed her, his mouth moving slowly over hers. Then he drew back a little and looked at her.

Her hair, a beautiful tangle of gold, was spread over the pillow, just as he had imagined it. Her eyes were deep pools of violet-blue.

Her face glowed.

It pleased him to know that he, his lovemaking, was the reason for that glow.

"Bellissima," he murmured, but she was more than beautiful. There was a wildness to her. She was exotic. Untamed. A feral cat that would purr only at the stroke of a special hand.

His hand.

"Draco. What are you thinking?"

"I'm thinking that you are an amazing woman,

Anna Orsini." He gathered her into his arms, brushed his lips lightly over hers. "And I'm very glad I came here tonight."

"So am I. Very glad you came here." She hesitated. "Not that I realized it until I opened the door and found you standing outside it, glowering at me."

He laughed softly.

"Glowering, huh?"

"Like a thundercloud."

"Well, I came here because I was angry."

"I know. I was, too."

"But then you opened the door and I saw you."

"All dressed up," Anna said, fluttering her lashes. "That designer robe. My hair in my eyes. And you couldn't resist me."

Draco grinned. Then his smile faded.

"And I knew I'd been lying to myself. That I'd come because I wanted you. I was just too thickheaded to see it."

"Too proud, you mean."

"No," he said quickly. Then he shrugged. "Maybe. Hell, not maybe. Yes. You're right." He kissed her, luxuriating in the sweetness of her mouth. "And you figured this out because...?"

"Because I can be the same sometimes. Proud. And a little arrogant." She sighed. "Which adds up to sometimes refusing to admit the truth to myself. See, you were supposed to be a chicken sandwich and a pot of tea."

"I am shocked, *bellissima,*" he said sternly, "shocked to learn that you were waiting for a chicken sandwich and not for me."

Anna laughed. "You aren't my type at all, you know."

"Well, you aren't mine. You're too beautiful, too sexy, too—"

"I'm serious."

She was. He could see it in her eyes.

"Because?"

"Because I'm not into arrogant, 'me Tarzan, you Jane' guys."

"Me? Arrogant?"

"You, Prince Valenti. Impossibly, egotistically arrogant." Her voice fell to a husky whisper. "And overdressed."

"Over...?" Draco laughed. She was right. She lay naked beneath him, but he was still wearing all his clothes. "You're right. But that's an easy problem to solve."

He rose to his feet, toed off his mocs, stripped off his clothes, watched her eyes darken when she saw that he was hard and erect again.

"Better now?" he said as he came down to her and gathered her in his arms.

"Much better. Much, much…"

He stopped her with a kiss. And then another kiss. He kissed his way down her throat, to her breasts, heard her breath catch as he sucked her nipples.

"Draco," she whispered, and he wrapped his fingers lightly around her wrists, lifted her hands to the bed's headboard, to its pale oak latticework.

"Hold on to that," he said gruffly, and he grasped her thighs and spread them wide. He looked at her for long seconds and then he gave a soft groan. "Such a perfect flower," he whispered, and he put his mouth to her and kissed her.

Anna cried out and jerked against the kiss, against the stroke of his tongue, and he slipped his hands beneath her, lifted her to him, sucked the sweet pink bud until she moaned with pleasure.

Yes, he thought. *Yes.* This was why he had come here tonight…

For her. For what she was, a woman with the heart and passion of a tigress.

For what she was, not who she was.

For her.

"Anna," he said, rising above her. "Anna," he demanded, "look at me."

Her eyes, dark and filled with a woman's mysteries, met his. When they did, he entered her. One long, hard thrust and he was deep inside her.

Together they set a rhythm as urgent as their need. Anna, sobbing, moved with him, moaning, her arms and legs wrapped around him.

"Draco," she said, "Draco…"

She felt her muscles begin to contract and she arched upward as she cried out.

His groan of release seemed to come from the depths of his soul.

She was weeping when he collapsed on top of her, tears of joy that he kissed away before rolling onto his back, taking her with him and holding her tightly against his heart.

Anna slept.

At least she thought she'd slept, because she opened her eyes and saw that the room was dark.

Someone had shut off the light. Drawn up the duvet that had been left, folded, at the foot of the bed.

No. Not "someone." Draco. She was in his arms, draped over him, skin to skin, her face against his throat, her hand splayed over his chest.

She could feel his heart beating slowly, steadily against hers.

Amazing, that she had fallen asleep in his arms. Amazing, that she had fallen asleep at all. She never slept after sex.

Well, yes. Of course she did, but never in a lover's arms.

After sex she liked to lie quietly with her lover for a while. They might talk or cuddle, and then she'd say that it was getting late and she had a busy day tomorrow, or whatever it took to remind the man it was time to leave her bed.

At least she'd stayed true to form for that. This was a hotel bed, but it was hers for tonight. And when a relationship reached the point where having sex was part of it, she wanted it to be in her own bed.

Not the man's.

It wasn't a rule or anything—it was just the way it was.

You brought a man into your bed, you remained in charge. You could tell him when it was time to go; you didn't have to suffer the ignominy of walking past a doorman, of getting into a taxi at eight in the morning wearing what you'd worn the night before.

And you avoided the kind of situation that might lead to a lover thinking you wanted the forevermore thing.

Anna had seen the forevermore thing, close up. Her father dominating her mother's very existence. Her mother living the life of a second-class citizen.

Start to finish, you were the one in control when the bed you slept in belonged to you.

Men had an intuitive understanding of that basic fact.

She'd once overheard her brothers talking as they lazed around in the conservatory of the Orsini mansion, drinking beer and BS-ing with an eye on the clock after some family occasion none of them had wanted to attend.

They were guys, and not married back then, so the conversation eventually got around to women.

Anna, hidden in the depths of an oversize wing chair, had started to stand up and tell them they might want to curtail the chatter until she was out of earshot, but before she could, Rafe had said he'd been thinking.

"Thinking," Dante had said. "You?"

"About, you know, what would be the perfect woman," Rafe had said, ignoring the dig. "Like, if she stayed the night, she wouldn't help herself to my razor to shave her legs."

There'd been murmurs of agreement all around.

"Right," Nick had said, "and she'd carry her own toothbrush in her purse."

"And she wouldn't want conversation in the morning," Dante had added.

That had elicited a grunt from Falco, Anna remembered wryly.

"What you guys mean is that the perfect woman would appear in your bed when you needed her, and disappear like Tinker Bell when you didn't."

The others had laughed like loons, which was the only reason Anna had risen from her chair.

"Whoa," Nick had said, and Anna had said

that *whoa* was exactly right, that what men really wanted were real-life versions of those vinyl blow-up dolls.

All her brothers had turned beet-red, and after she'd had a good laugh at the sight, she'd told them that she had a big surprise for them.

"Women want the same thing," she'd said. "A guy who'd show up in bed when you needed him and then vanish."

If there was a shade that went past beet-red, her brothers had achieved it.

"You're just trying to embarrass us," the usually non-embarrassable Falco had sputtered.

Well, no.

She hadn't been trying to do that—she'd simply been speaking honestly.

Women liked sex, too. At least, most of them did.

It was just that women were brought up to think that good girls never admitted it or, at the very least, good girls wrapped sex with pink ribbons.

Not her.

She didn't believe in sleeping around—talk about misnomers!—but that didn't mean you couldn't be honest about what you wanted. And what you didn't want.

And what Anna didn't want, ever, was one man, one woman, that whole foolish thing called forevermore...

Which brought her back to basics.

It was time to wake Draco, tell him this had been wonderful but it was late, she had a full day ahead of her tomorrow and it was time he went home.

Of course, that wouldn't be news to him. The full-day-tomorrow part. He knew it, because he was going to be part of that day.

Great sex or not, they hadn't settled anything. He still owned land she'd come here to claim.

Anna nearly groaned.

How could she have forgotten that? Since when did she let emotion get in the way of logic?

What she'd told Draco was true. She'd been attracted to him from the start, even though she'd denied it until tonight. Seeing him at her door had forced her to face the truth, that even while she'd said she despised him, she'd wanted to go to bed with him.

Okay. Desire was one thing, but violating her

ethical role in this situation was very much another issue.

She was an attorney, and attorneys didn't get involved with the respondents in their cases. Assuming there would be a case to be involved in.

Okay. She'd made a mistake, a big one, but there was no sense in dwelling on it. What mattered was that it would not happen again.

The sex had been good, but she'd had good sex before...

"Hey."

Startled, Anna raised her head and looked at Draco, who gave her a slow, sexy smile.

"You're up," she said brightly. "Good. I mean, I was just going to wake you."

He shifted his weight, rolled her onto her back and framed her face with his hands.

"And just how were you planning on doing that?"

The sound of his voice sent a tremor dancing along her spine.

"Draco," she said, "listen to me."

"This was a mistake."

"Yes. Yes, it was. I'm glad you understand—"

He kissed her, his lips moving against hers with

slow, heart-stopping deliberation. She wanted to return the kiss, wrap herself in his heat, but she knew better than to give in.

"Please listen, Draco. I'm trying to tell you that—"

"We're on opposite sides of what might become a lawsuit."

"Exactly. And—"

"That makes us enemies."

Anna sighed with relief. "Yes. This was…it was nice, but—"

"Nice?" he said, his voice a low growl.

"More than nice. It was—"

He kissed her again, deeper, more intensely. She felt him harden against her, felt that hot, electric jolt racing from her belly to her breasts.

Oh no, she thought, no, this wasn't just good sex, it was something much more. She'd never felt this way before, as if she were standing at the edge of forever.

Draco slid into her. Her breath caught. Helpless, drowning in pleasure, she cried out as she rose toward him.

"Tell me to stop," he said thickly, "and I will."

She stared up into his dark eyes.

"All you have to do is say the words, Anna."

"All right." She ran the tip of her tongue over her lips. "I want—I want—"

Anna moaned, tunneled her fingers into his hair and brought Draco's mouth to hers.

A long time later she stirred, rolled to her side and nestled back against him.

"I meant to tell you," she said drowsily, "you don't have to worry. I'm on the pill."

"Bene." He curved his arm around her, his hand cupping her breast. "Otherwise, I would have to leave you and go in search of a pharmacy." He nipped the nape of her neck. "And that would be a pitiful sight, *bellissima,* a grown man crawling on his hands and knees through the nighttime streets of Rome."

Anna laughed.

And tumbled into the dark cavern of sleep.

CHAPTER EIGHT

REALITY came back in the blurred rush of gray morning light seeping through the sheer drapes, the soft patter of rain...

And the pressure of a man's muscular arm curved around Anna's waist.

Disoriented, she closed her eyes, concentrated....

And remembered everything.

Draco. The thrill of opening her door and finding him there. The shimmering flash of excitement at what she saw in his face, the realization that she had wanted him all along, that half her anger at him was really anger at herself for wanting a man like him.

The night had been... What word could possibly sum it up? Incredible. Fantastic. Electric with passion so powerful it had turned her brain to jelly.

How else to explain why he was still in her bed?

She could make sense of having fallen asleep in his arms that first time. Combine exhaustion with the out-of-body feeling she always got from jet lag, and anything was possible.

She'd gone through that list of explanations hours ago.

But she'd done it again. Gone to sleep in his arms so soundly that she couldn't even recall it happening.

Surprise number one, for sure.

And added to that, surprise number two.

Why had he stayed? He could have left any time during the night. From what she knew of men, given a choice, that was the way they preferred it.

No man wanted the morning-after thing, that series of dance steps that could be far more complicated than the dance a man and woman had just performed in bed a couple of hours before.

Stilted chitchat. The "after you, no, that's fine, after you" shower routine. A guy's unattractive early-morning stubble, a woman's totally unappealing bed-head hairstyle.

Hers was, for sure. Lots of curls, no sleek

smoothness, just unruly locks that were wild and, without question, awful looking.

The entire morning-after scenario was enough to ruin romance as a concept, for lack of a better phrase. The truth was, good sex didn't have anything much to do with romance. It had to do with physical attraction. And hormones. A certain look in a man's eyes, a certain way he touched you.

If he was right and the time was right, that was all you needed. Given those basics, a woman was ready.

Anna shifted her weight just a little.

Draco felt so good spooned against her.

And she'd been ready. Hell, ready and waiting even when she hadn't known what she'd been ready and waiting for.

Draco Valenti was one gorgeous hunk.

And as it turned out, he was spectacular in bed. He knew what to touch and how to touch it; he knew when to whisper and when to keep silent; he knew when to take charge—yes, he certainly did—and when to let a woman take the lead.

And she was turning herself on.

Ridiculous, because one of the other reasons

she didn't like sleeping with a man all night was that men always wanted morning sex as part of The Morning Thing, and Anna had never been a morning-sex fan.

Bottom line? Good sex was, well, it was good sex. Yes, she had to like a guy to have sex with him. Had to enjoy his company, but sex was sex. Women who didn't understand that were in for trouble.

They fell in love.

They got married.

And, surprise surprise, they ended up hurt.

Anna, fortunately, was not, would never be, one of those women.

She and Isabella had talked about it just a few months ago.

They'd met for lunch at a place they both liked in midtown, poking at salads and drinking Diet Cokes, playing catch-up because they hadn't seen each other in a couple of weeks. Izzy had asked about a guy Anna had been seeing, if maybe she was serious about him, and Anna had rolled her eyes and said what was there to be serious about?

He was fun, he was interesting, he was good in bed.

"End of story," she'd told Iz. "Why would I want to spoil things?"

Izzy had put down her fork and heaved one of her Izzy sighs, the kind you could imagine a fairy princess giving while she waited for her Prince Charming to appear.

"That's such a sad attitude, Anna. What about love?"

"What about it?" Anna had replied, spearing a grape tomato and popping it into her mouth. "You have to stop reading all those women's magazines stuffed with that June, moon, forever-after bull."

Izzy had sighed again. "Honestly, Anna, I don't know what you're trying to prove."

"Nothing. Women don't need to prove anything. Well, maybe only that we're women, not idiots. You don't really think only men are entitled to be realistic about these things? About sex?"

Iz had shaken her head and Anna had smiled benignly, and they'd gone on to safer ground—Anna's defense of a woman who'd shoplifted a winter jacket for her little boy because she didn't have the money to buy one, and Izzy's plans for the garden she was designing for a friend.

The thing was, Izzy's lovely head was in the clouds.

Anna's was right here, squarely on her shoulders.

She liked her space the same way men liked theirs, which brought her straight back to the fact that Draco was still in her bed and she was still in his arms and—

"Buon giorno, bellissima."

She tried to think of some clever reply, but she couldn't come up with anything. "Good morning" was deliciously sexy in his husky Italian, but it was only "good morning" in American English.

"How did you sleep?"

Deeply. Soundly. Who wouldn't sleep that way after what had happened that last time they'd made—that last time they'd had sex?

All she remembered were Draco's kisses, his caresses, his hard length deep, deep inside her and a rush of exquisite sensation, a breathless moment when the world spun out of control—and then the feel of him drawing her back into the warm, secure cradle of his body…

"Anna."

Draco's voice was low and rough. Just the sound of it made her skin tingle. And when he slid his hand up her side and cupped her breast...

Physiology, she told herself, that was what it was. He was a wonderful lover. Any woman would react to his touch even when she knew it was time to put the night in perspective.

"Anna," he said again, and turned her toward him.

Her heartbeat stuttered. He was gorgeous. Why had she ever thought early-morning stubble unattractive? It was perfect, the absolutely proper accent note to his square jaw, that magnificent Roman nose, the dark, dark eyes.

He smiled.

Anna almost flinched.

Why wouldn't he smile? She probably looked like a wild woman.

"Beautiful Anna," he said softly, and he threaded his fingers through her awful, scrunched-up hair and brought his mouth to hers.

The kiss was long. And tender.

It wasn't at all what she expected.

Her couple of experiences of The Morning Thing involved one kind of kiss.

A kiss that was a prelude to morning sex.

Which, as she had already established, was not her thing at all.

But this kiss was.

It was soft. Undemanding. A sweet meeting of lips, of tongues…

"Stop analyzing," Draco whispered.

Anna jerked back.

"What do you mean? I am not analy—"

"*Sì, Signorina Avocato.* You are." He drew her to him, his lips curved in a smile. "You're being an attorney, trying to decide what to say. What to do. And you're struggling for answers to questions. Why did we make love? Why did he spend the night? Why did I permit it?" He kissed her again. "This is not a courtroom, Anna."

Anna couldn't help smiling. "And a good thing it isn't."

"I agree, for if it were a courtroom…" Draco rolled her onto her back. "If it were, I could not do this."

"Oh. Oh…"

"Or this."

Her lashes drooped to her cheeks. "Draco," she whispered, "Draco, wait…"

He kissed her, and this kiss was not tender or soft—it was hot and urgent. So was the play of his fingers on her breast. And when he parted her thighs, brought his mouth to her core, Anna cried out, reached for her lover, rose to him and impaled herself on his rigid flesh.

It turned out that there was no problem with bed-head hair.

"Don't look at me," Anna said a long time later when Draco wanted to do exactly that. "I'm a mess."

His dark eyebrows rose.

"You think so?" he said, and when she nodded, he scooped her into his arms, carried her to the bathroom and stood her before the full-length mirror. "Look," he said, and when Anna groaned and tried to turn away, he wouldn't let her. "Look," he demanded in a tone she'd learned meant he wouldn't take no for an answer.

So she looked—and saw herself, her hair a tousled mass of gold curls, her mouth pink and gently swollen, her breasts still rosy from her last orgasm.

She saw the faint blue bruises on her thighs

where Draco had nipped her flesh, then soothed it with kisses; saw a matching mark on her throat...

Saw him standing behind her, his arms cradling her.

God, how beautiful he was. How incredibly masculine. How big and powerful and...

Her breath caught as he cupped her breasts, played with her nipples as his eyes grew dark as the night.

Watching him, watching herself, was the most erotic thing Anna had ever done.

He bent his head, nuzzled aside the curls from the nape of her neck and kissed her skin, then kissed the juncture of her neck and shoulder. She moaned, reached between them and encircled as much as she could of his rigid, straining erection.

A growl rose in his throat; his teeth sank into her flesh and she cried out in passion.

"Hold on to the vanity, *bellissima*," he said thickly, his hands clasping her hips. "*Sì*. Just like that..."

She sobbed his name, came apart the instant he entered her. She heard his cry, felt him shudder and the world shattered again.

Draco's arms swept around her. She fell back

against his hard body, trembling, her legs bone-less. He held her as their heartbeats steadied, his face buried in her hair, and then he turned her to him, enfolded her in his embrace, held her close as his big hands stroked up and down her spine.

"Are you all right?" he whispered.

Anna nodded. He lifted her face to his, brushed his lips lightly over hers. Then he scooped her off her feet and carried her into the shower.

He washed her. She washed him. It was a game at first; how could it have been anything else after what had just happened?

But their hands moved more and more slowly, found more and more places to soap and gently, carefully wash until Draco groaned, leaned his forehead against Anna's and said, "I hope the maid has a strong heart."

Anna looked up at him. "Why?"

"When she finds us in here, waterlogged… Well, you and I will have died happy, but I doubt if she will."

Anna laughed. Draco grinned, turned off the shower, grabbed a bath sheet and wrapped her in it.

"You think that's funny, Orsini?" he said,

trying his damnedest to sound stern. He didn't feel stern, not even jokingly so. He felt…he felt happy, and though he'd felt a lot of different things after sex, *happy* wasn't a word he'd have used to describe any of them.

"You have to admit," Anna said, "it's an, um, an interesting image."

"What is?" he said, and then he remembered what he'd said about the housekeeper and he laughed and tipped her chin up. "Where's your compassion?"

"Where's yours?" she said, teasing him right back. "A compassionate man would have phoned down for coffee by now."

"You're right," he said solemnly as he spun her toward the door, then patted her lightly on the backside. "Get into your robe while I order breakfast."

Anna looked at him. "Was that an order, Valenti? Because you need to know I don't follow orders."

Her tone was still teasing, but there was a quick flash of fire in her eyes. *Dio,* Draco thought, this was one hell of a woman.

"No?"

"No."

"We'll see about that," he said huskily, and he took her mouth in another long, deep kiss.

Breakfast arrived.

And somewhere between the fresh fruit and the coffee, reality once again began its inevitable claim.

I don't follow orders, she'd said.

And Draco had answered, *We'll see about that.*

Meaningless banter… Or was it?

Those were not the words you wanted to hear from your adversary.

That was who Draco Valenti was. Her adversary. She'd come to Rome to deal with him. Instead, she'd slept with him.

She'd even told him to order breakfast.

It was such a silly mental segue that Anna almost laughed…. But she didn't. This was her room. She should have phoned down for the meal. Why let a man do what she could and should do for herself?

She looked at Draco, sprawled back against the pillows in a matching hotel robe, his dark-as-midnight hair still damp, his skin tanned and golden against the white linens.

Was this what came of letting your lover spend the entire night in your bed?

Actually, he wasn't her lover. They had no relationship apart from what had happened last night and this morning.

What she'd let happen.

Okay. So she'd broken a rule. Let him spend the night. Well, no. She'd broken two rules. She shouldn't have had sex with him in the first place. This was no different than being in a courtroom.

Would she sleep with the prosecutor? And hadn't she had the discussion with herself already? She had. Then how had this happened? How had she let this man make her forget such basic principles?

"A penny," Draco said in that low, husky voice of his. Anna raised her eyebrows and played dumb. He smiled. "For your thoughts."

He had an amazing smile.

Tender. Sexy. Masculine. She felt its effects straight down to her toes. Even looking at him looking at her made her feel…well, it made her feel strange.

As if she'd lost her equilibrium. Or something.

It was unsettling. She didn't like it. Or maybe she liked it too much, and what in heck was that supposed to mean?

"Anna?" He put his coffee cup on the night-stand and sat up straight. "What is it?"

Anna cleared her throat.

"Nothing. I mean—I mean, I was just think-ing…. Perhaps this would be a good time to agree on what happens next."

He grinned. It made her pulse stutter.

"An excellent suggestion, *cara*." He took her cup from her hands and set it beside his. His fin-gers brushed hers. She fought the sudden urge to fling herself into his arms.

What in the world is wrong with you, Orsini? Are you losing your mind?

"I suspect we can think of something," he said.

"No." Her voice was breathy, the kind of old-fashioned I'm-just-a-girl-and-you're-such-a-sexy-stud thing she despised in women. "No," she said, briskly this time, and drew back her hand. "I didn't mean it that way."

His eyes focused on hers. "What way did you mean it?"

Anna wished she were not wearing a robe, not sitting on a bed rumpled from a night of sex, not facing a man who looked as if he had just stepped out of *GQ*.

"I meant…well, I was thinking that—that I hope you understand, this was, uh, it was fine."

His eyes narrowed to obsidian slits.

"Fine?" he said softly, and Anna winced.

"It was great."

"Great," he said even more softly.

She was digging herself into a hole. She took a breath, forced what she hoped was a brilliant smile.

"You know what I mean. It was—it was—"

"What was, Anna? Breakfast? The coffee?" A muscle knotted in his jaw. "Or are you speaking of what happened between us in this bed?"

Now she was blushing. She knew it. And what was there to blush about?

He folded his arms over his chest.

"Let me save you the trouble. You were thinking that the sex had nothing to do with our situation."

"Yes," she said quickly. "I'm glad you understand. We're still adversaries."

He said nothing. Perhaps he hadn't understood her. His English seemed flawless but, as an attorney, especially one who worked with the poor, she often dealt with people who seemed to speak excellent English and yet still struggled with words that had a particular subtlety to them.

"You know," she said carefully. "The land."

He went on looking at her, saying nothing. A muscle ticked in his jaw; she saw it and she stood up to gain whatever advantage it might give her.

"Look, I'm simply trying to set things straight. We slept together."

"Such a charming phrase."

"Why? Because it comes from a woman?"

Draco's lips drew back from his teeth. "It comes from the Orsini *consigliere.*"

Anna's chin came up. "You're twisting my words."

"Then let me untwist them. You're telling me that we had sex. And I should not assume the event was a turning point in our little legal drama."

His voice was more than flat; it was as cold as winter. Anna moistened her lips with the tip of her tongue.

"I wouldn't have put it quite so—so—"

"Bluntly?" He stood up, and she lost whatever pathetic advantage in height she'd had.

"Well, yes. I mean—"

"You mean," he said with a quick, sharp smile, "I should not think that by sleeping with me, you've given up your right to try and take from me that which is mine."

There it was again, all that upper-class arrogance. That I-am-rich-and-you-are-not rubbish that had driven her parents from Sicily, that she saw every day in her work.

"The land is not yours, and you damned well know it!"

"It is mine, it has always been mine, and no Sicilian thug is going to change that by sending his daughter to do his dirty work in her bed."

"You—you aristocratic bastard!"

"Tell me, Anna. Whose idea was it to sleep with the enemy? Yours? Or your father's?"

Anna's hand flew through the air and cracked against Draco's jaw. He caught her by the wrist, twisted her arm behind her, brought her to her toes.

"Did you really think I would tell you that I

changed my mind? That I would be happy to let you have the land in exchange for me having had you?"

"That's disgusting!"

"What is disgusting," he said in a low voice, "is that I should have forgotten, even for a moment, that the blood of thieves and thugs runs in your veins."

"Get out," she snapped. "Get the hell out of my room!"

His hand fell from hers. "With pleasure," he said, turning his back and reaching for his clothes.

"Just get this straight," Anna said, her voice shaking with anger. "The Orsinis will see to it that you'll never be able to use that land, not if I have to stay here for the next hundred years."

He turned toward her just as his robe fell open.

Her heartbeat stuttered.

Naked, he was as dangerous looking as he was beautiful. The wide shoulders, leanly muscled torso and long legs. And the part of him that was male, that she knew so intimately, knew was almost frighteningly potent…

The air in the room seemed to turn thick and still.

Anna's gaze flew to Draco's face. She could hear the pulse of her blood beating in her ears. Neither of them moved until, at last, he gave a harsh laugh.

"You flatter yourself, *bellissima.* I have had my fill of what you so generously offered." Slowly, confidently he dressed, then strolled to the door. "I'll return for you in an hour. Be ready. I don't like to be kept waiting."

"Ready for what?"

"Ready to deal with our mutual problem so that we can see the last of each other."

Anna moved toward him. "Just tell me where to meet you. I absolutely forbid you to—"

"Was that an order, Orsini?" His smile was as thin as the blade of a knife. "Because you have to know I don't follow orders."

"Listen, Valenti—"

"No," he snarled, "*you* listen! I will be back in an hour, *il mio consigliere.* And if you have anything in your luggage besides those lady lawyer suits and ridiculous stilettos, I suggest you wear them."

"You're despicable," Anna said. "Absolutely des—"

Draco caught her by the wrist, hauled her to him and stopped the angry flow of words with a merciless kiss.

Then he was gone.

CHAPTER NINE

THE hotel doorman was not the same one as last night.

He looked shocked when Draco asked for his Ferrari.

A Ferrari? Here? No. That was impossible. Surely the *signore* could see that this was not a hotel at which anyone would leave such an automobile.

True enough.

The place was clean, but that was about it. Apparently, Cesare Orsini didn't believe in providing his *consigliere* with a decent expense account.

Draco, fighting an anger he knew was meant for that *consigliere* and not for the pudgy fool dressed like an extra in a bad operetta, agreed.

The hotel was not the place for a Ferrari.

Nonetheless, he said, he had left *his* Ferrari here, at the curb, last evening. And as he said it, he took a hundred-euro note from his wallet and handed it over.

Ah, the doorman said, palming the bill, how could he have forgotten? He snapped his fingers, pointed at a pimply-faced kid wearing what Draco figured was a bellman's costume, and sent the boy running. Seconds later the car was at the curb. Draco tipped the kid and got behind the wheel, burning rubber as he peeled away.

The intersection ahead was a typical snarl of traffic, cars and taxis and motorcycles growling like jungle beasts in anticipation of the green light and the chance to cut each other off.

Draco floored the gas, steered between a truck and a taxi, skidded around a motorcycle, got to the front of the pack just as the light changed and kept going. It won him a chorus of angry-sounding horns. A joke, considering that obeying traffic laws was pretty much against Roman law.

Too bad one of the drivers didn't feel like making something of it. That big guy on the black Augusta motorcycle, for example. Hell, if he was looking for trouble…

Dio.

Draco was the one looking for trouble, and for what reason? A woman he'd slept with had said something that had angered him. If he had a hundred euros for every female who'd ever said anything that had irritated him...

But this had gone beyond irritation. Anna's suggestion, hell, her assumption that he'd figure the night they'd spent had changed the fact that they had a dispute to settle was insulting.

He had to put it out of his head.

Draco stepped down harder on the gas. The mood he was in, driving fast was safer than thinking, but how could a man stop thinking?

His head felt as if it might explode.

Damn Anna Orsini. Damn himself, too. How could he have forgotten that old saw about never mixing business with pleasure?

That he had just didn't make sense.

Anna was attractive. So what? He knew dozens, scores of attractive women. Why be modest at a moment like this? Attractive women, beautiful women were his for the taking.

Hadn't he just left one behind in Hawaii? In fact, he thought coldly, if you wanted to be blunt about it, Giselle was the better looking of the two.

Maybe not.

Maybe she was just more interested in pleasing him than Anna was.

Giselle was always perfumed, every hair in place, her face carefully made-up even when he knew she'd spent who knew how long making sure she didn't look made-up. He'd been with her for, what, two months? In all that time he'd never seen her looking disheveled unless it was artfully so.

Sometimes he suspected she slipped from bed so she could tiptoe into the bathroom to fix her hair and face before he woke and saw her.

Anna certainly hadn't bothered to do that.

By morning her hair had been a wild tangle, her lipstick a memory. She had not looked even remotely perfect.

Draco's hands tightened on the steering wheel.

She'd looked like a woman who had enjoyed every moment she'd spent in her lover's arms, but if that were true, would she even have thought of pointing out that their dispute was not settled just because they'd had sex?

Was there nothing on her mind but that cursed land in Sicily?

Probably not.

A woman with so much attitude… *Dio,* she was impossible. She had an opinion on everything. She was stubborn and defiant, and she argued at the drop of a hat.

He had to have been out of his mind to have slept with her.

Not that he preferred his women to be compliant.

He was not a male chauvinist—he was just a man who understood that men were men and women were women, and a little show of deference to the dominant sex, goddamnit, could be a very nice thing.

He was still driving too fast, but the traffic had lessened. That was one of the benefits of living off the Via Appia Antica. A handful of villas, lots of parkland, lots of space.

And space, metaphorically speaking, was what he needed right now.

Unbelievable that Anna would think of the land first and the hours they'd spent making love a distant second.

Correction again.

They hadn't made love.

They'd had sex. Anna had been very clear about that, and rightly so. That ability to see sex as a man saw it was definitely one thing he liked about her.

Making love was a woman's phrase, a female way of twisting words to turn something basic and honest into something they could do without having to admit they had the same appetites as men.

Men spoke of making love, but the truth was that as far as they were concerned, "making love" was a euphemism for a four-letter word or, in polite company, a three-letter one.

S-e-x.

It was what men and women did in bed. It was what he and Anna had done. In bed, and out of it. Against the wall, with her legs wrapped around him. Against the vanity, with his hands on her hips. In the shower, with the soap turning their skin slick...

Was he insane? He had to be, or why would he be driving along at a zillion miles an hour and turning himself on with hot images of a woman he was sorry he'd ever met?

The gates to his villa loomed ahead. Draco slowed the Ferrari, depressed a button and the gates swung slowly open.

The point was they'd had sex. And then she'd brought them both down to earth by accusing him of figuring the night they'd spent together might have been a *quid pro quo.*

What it had been, he thought grimly as he pulled up before the villa and killed the engine, what it had been was pure, raw hunger.

It had filled him, nearly consumed him, though he'd refused to admit it, even to himself, until Anna had opened the hotel door, looking beautiful without makeup, with her hair a sexy tumble of untamed curls; looking delicate and strong— and no way was he going to try to figure out how a woman could seem strong and fragile at the same time.

Anna did, that was all.

She was too complex for her own good and certainly for his, and knowing that, he'd still wanted her.

And she had wanted him just as intensely, just

as passionately, even though he was supposed to be her enemy.

She had an honest, open attitude toward sex. He liked that about her, too. And damnit, it was ridiculous to fault her for putting into words what a man might well have thought—that maybe being intimate had put an end to their legal dispute.

Only a man would think that way. Or, at least, speak so bluntly.

Was that what this was all about?

Was he angry because Anna Orsini was a gorgeous, desirable woman, never mind all that nonsense about her simply being attractive, who spoke a man's thoughts and expressed a man's hunger? He'd never dealt with a woman like her before.

Did it make him uncomfortable?

Or did it go beyond that?

Was it because in some deep, dark foolish part of him, he wanted to know if she was like this with other men? Was she as ready, as hot, as wet for them as she had been for him?

Not that he gave a damn…

Draco slapped his hands against the steering wheel.

There was no logic to it. There could not be any logic to it. He'd made a mistake, and that was that.

He should never have permitted the controversy with Cesare Orsini to go this far. He should have ignored that last letter. Failing that, he should not have gone ahead and met with Orsini's representative without his own lawyer present.

But he had, and now he'd compounded the mess by sleeping with Anna.

He was tired of the nonsense. Of all of it. A thug who had spent his life stealing from others and thought he could go on doing it. A woman who thought he might see sex as a bargaining tool…

Draco narrowed his eyes.

Was that the real purpose of that little speech? Had she hoped that he truly had seen the night as a kind of trade? She'd given him a night to remember; he would give her the land?

Hold on, a voice inside him said, *she never even suggested that. It was you, dummy. You haven't just leaped to a conclusion, you arrived in that fantasyland all by yourself. And you didn't just arrive there, you landed with both feet. Remem-*

ber what you said about her doing her father's dirty work in her bed?

A mess. At total, stinking mess.

Draco got out of the car and slammed the door behind him.

Who cared who had done what? He'd had enough of the Orsinis, father and daughter.

By nightfall he'd be rid of them both.

Anna had packed lightly for her trip to Rome.

Two suits. Four white silk blouses. Three pairs of heels, and what had that full-of-himself fool meant by calling her stilettos 'ridiculous'?

"You try going without lunch for four months to buy a pair," she muttered as she pawed through the clothes she'd brought with her.

Better still, let him try wearing them.

The picture that leaped into her head, Draco attempting to stuff his big feet into her size sevens, might have made her laugh if she'd been in a laughing mood. But she wasn't, not even over the Cinderella story told in reverse.

Besides, no matter how you turned things around, Prince Valenti was no Prince Charming.

He was an aristocratic, autocratic idiot, she

thought grimly. And if she owed him for anything, it was that he'd gone out of his way to remind her of it.

Such an overreaction to her simple statement about them still being adversaries. How could you insult a man by telling him the truth?

Or maybe that was the problem. Maybe the truth was that he'd figured he was so good in bed that he'd dazzled her into giving up what had brought her to Rome in the first place.

Anna rolled her eyes as she searched through her clothes.

That would never work with her. She wasn't a girlish fool who'd lose her girlish heart over him just because she'd slept with him, and what was with the silly euphemism?

They hadn't slept together—they'd had sex. That's what it always was to a man, and to any woman with a functional brain.

One of the things Anna loved about the law was that it had the right words to describe whatever needed describing.

Sex was like that.

Why pretend? Why give the act fanciful names that had to do with sleeping or, even worse, with romance? Why make it sound as if the heart was involved in a strictly biological act?

As for her pointing out that a night of sex had not changed the bottom line... The almighty prince might not like hearing the truth, but people traded sex for what they really wanted all the time. Her professional life was full of examples. Sad-eyed women staying with men who beat them, just so they could have roofs over their heads. Gorgeous models married grotesque old men so they could wallow in money and jewels.

Anna's mouth thinned.

There were other kinds of trades, too. Look at the one her own mother had made.

Sofia Orsini stayed with her gangster husband so that she wouldn't have to face the disgrace that went with an old-fashioned Sicilian woman asking for a divorce. What other explanation could there possibly be?

Anna slapped her hands on her hips and blew a curl off her forehead.

Well, she wasn't like that.

She didn't need a man to keep her housed, clothed and fed. She didn't want jewels or anything she couldn't afford to buy for herself. And she sure as hell would divorce a bastard who deserved divorce, except she'd never have to.

Marriage, a lifetime commitment, was absolutely not on her agenda.

She liked men, liked spending time with them, liked having sex on occasion, but all on her own straightforward terms. No trading. No promises. No lies.

Love was an illusion. Sex was sex, and what did any of that have to do with the ugly little scene here a few minutes ago?

She'd made a candid statement. How had Draco managed to make it sound, well, cheap? It wasn't. It had been honest, that was all.

The prince didn't like honesty? Too bad.

And she wasn't going to forget that accusation he'd hurled at her. Suggesting she'd gone to bed with him to change his mind about the land...

That had hurt. Because making love with him... No. Having sex with him had been, it had been...

"Damnit," Anna said, her voice shaking.

Never mind thinking about what had happened.

It was time to look forward.

And where were the jeans, the T, the sneakers she knew she'd packed? She always brought along stuff like that. Getting snowed in at an airport in upstate New York on a ski trip her senior year in law school had taught her two things.

One, she hated skiing.

Two, when you flew anywhere, you always had to pack something comfortable to wear.

And there were the things she'd been looking for, tucked on a shelf in the tiny hotel-room closet. Old jeans. Older sneakers. An ancient T-shirt that she positively adored.

Who wouldn't?

This was not any T, it was the one Isabella had given her on her last birthday. It was vintage, from the 1970s. Isabella said she'd found it in a little shop in Soho. The shirt was gray and slightly faded, but the words that marched across the front of it read loud and clear.

A Woman Needs a Man Like a Fish Needs a Bicycle.

Truer words had never graced a T-shirt.

Anna took off the robe, pulled on a bra and

panties, stepped into the jeans, zipped them up and tugged the shirt over her head.

The jeans rode low on her hips; the shirt was a little short.

She looked in the mirror. Her belly button showed. Maybe she'd get it pierced when she got home.

Too bad she hadn't done it sooner. Then she'd be wearing the perfect outfit for Draco's stuffy office because, of course, that was where he was taking her.

Did he think the formal setting would intimidate her?

The hell it would.

Neither would whatever he intended to say.

She wasn't finished with this fight. There were courts here, just as there were back home, and Cesare had all the money she'd need for translators, lawyers, the works.

Plus, just as she'd warned Draco, there was the ever-voracious press. He was right—her father would not want the publicity. But who cared what Cesare wanted? He'd sent her here. How she handled things was her business.

Anna grabbed her purse.

Forget going home tomorrow. She would stay in Rome as long as it took to recoup her mother's land.

She didn't know how she'd pull it off, not yet, but she would.

After that, Prince Draco Marcellus Valenti could go straight to hell.

CHAPTER TEN

DRACO saw Anna the minute he pulled his car to the curb outside the hotel.

She was standing a few feet away, highlighted by the watery sun that had appeared after the rain, and he could see that she'd taken his advice.

No lady lawyer suit. No killer heels. She wore jeans, sneakers, a T-shirt. What did the shirt say? He squinted, read it…and knew he was in for a long day.

At least she looked like an average woman.

The hell she did.

There was nothing average about her. It was all pure Anna, from the straight-as-an-arrow posture to the defiant set of her chin, from the tips of those well-worn and, he was sure, definitely unfashionable sneakers to the gold curls that were already trying to spring free of whatever it was she'd used to tie them back.

What was it he'd thought before? Delicate but strong—and so what?

He wanted her gone, and by tomorrow she would be.

The guy in the Gilbert and Sullivan get-up spotted him, saw Anna begin marching toward him and rushed past her, his obvious goal to score points by reaching the car before she did.

Anna offered a stony glare and a dismissive wave of her hand.

All she had to add was a thumbs-down gesture and a lion would surely have appeared to sink its fangs into the poor guy and drag him away.

And then there was that T-shirt. Never mind the way her breasts thrust against the thin cotton, or the way it clung to her skin. It was the message written across it that got him, that woman-bicycle-fish thing.

For some crazy reason it made him want to drag her into the car and kiss her until she wound her arms around his neck and begged him to make love to her—except it wasn't love, it was, just as she'd pointed out, sex.

"You find this amusing?" she demanded.

Draco turned what threatened to be a grin into a scowl.

"Nothing about you is amusing, Orsini." He leaned across the front seat and pushed the door open. "Get in."

"Perhaps you didn't get my message. I don't need you to open doors. I am perfectly capable of doing things for myself."

Her voice rang with icy scorn. Draco narrowed his eyes. The lady needed some lessons in manners, and for the few hours she'd still be annoyingly at his side he was damned well going to be the one teaching them to her.

"Forgive me," he said, his voice as chilly as hers. "For a moment I forgot how you feel about good manners."

Her face went pink. Good, he thought grimly. In fact, excellent.

"As for your treatment of the doorman, he was simply trying to do his job."

"A useless job."

"A job," Draco said. "Something that puts food on the table, though I doubt if someone in your situation would ever have to worry about that."

Anna felt her color deepen.

He was right, of course, though what a prince would know about putting food on the table was beyond her.

She certainly knew what it was like. How it felt to worry about money. When you refused financial support from your father to get you through university, when you lied to your brothers and said thanks but you didn't need any help paying your tuition, your room, your board...

"You going to get in the car or not? Make up your mind, *consigliere*. I'm not in the mood for games."

What she wanted to do was slam the door in his handsome, arrogant face, but, speaking of jobs, she had one to do and she was going to do it.

Anna tossed her head, slid into the passenger seat and flashed a sickly-sweet smile at the doorman when he reached, warily, for the door.

"Grazie," she said, but when she looked at Draco, the saccharine smile faded. "You," she said, each letter a virtual pellet of ice, "would, of course, be fully cognizant of what it's like to worry about putting food on the table."

Draco thought back to the years he'd spent eating one meal a day so he could put most of what he earned into paying for the exorbitant costs of getting his degree—well, of almost getting that degree—but he'd never told anyone about those years and no way was he ever going to talk about it with someone like Anna Orsini.

Instead, he handed the doorman a tip and then stepped hard on the gas.

"Oh, I don't know," he said as the car shot away from the curb. "Truffles and caviar aren't always easy to find."

Anna glared at him. A joke? For all she knew, a statement of fact.

Not that she cared.

Her temper was at boiling point again, and there was nobody to blame but herself.

She despised Draco Valenti, yet she'd gone to bed with him. She was a modern woman, yes. But she was a discriminating woman. She did not go to bed with men she despised.

Now she was compounding that error by, heaven help her, obeying his regal commands.

What was she doing, sitting in his car like an obedient slave? Why was she letting him take her somewhere without knowing where that some-where was? Why had she not worn what he'd scoffingly referred to as her lady lawyer outfit? That's what she was. A lawyer, never mind the sexist and demeaning "lady" sobriquet.

And not to dwell on it or anything…

Why had she ever gone to bed with him?

Because you wanted to, a scathing voice inside her purred. *Because he's gorgeous and sexy, funny and smart. He's arrogant, too, and you love his unmitigated arrogance. You love it when he has the balls to stand up to you, love it even more when he takes you in his arms and changes everything you thought you knew about being with a man….*

"…change everything you thought you knew about it," Draco said.

Anna swung toward him, horrified. "I didn't mean to say…"

His eyebrows rose. Okay! She hadn't said anything. She was not so far out of touch with reality that she was speaking her thoughts out loud.

"Never mind," she said quickly. "I, uh, I was just—just thinking about something…."

Draco narrowed his eyes.

Thinking about what? he wondered.

Her eyes had gone blurry; her cheeks had

taken on a rosy glow. It reminded him of how she looked in the heat of passion, when he'd held her in his arms, her body warm and yielding as he moved inside her, her moans of ecstasy his, all his…

Damnit, he thought in righteous indignation, what was wrong with him?

"Forget thinking," he snapped, "and try paying attention. And I know it's difficult, but try having an open mind, okay?"

"About what?"

"About my land in Sicily."

"It's Orsini land."

Draco snorted. How had he forgotten, even for a second, that this was Anna Orsini, her father's *consigliere?* Anything else was just an illusion.

They rode in silence for a few minutes. Then Anna turned toward him, frowning.

"This isn't the way to your office."

"No," he said calmly. "It isn't."

"Then where are we going?"

"To a place where we can settle this idiocy."

"If you think I'm going to let you take me somewhere to try and seduce me—"

"Did anyone ever tell you that you have an over-blown opinion of yourself as a sexual trophy?"

"You," Anna said through her teeth, "are a horrible human being!"

Draco laughed. That only made her angrier. She was glaring at him, her lips set in a thin, angry line. What would she do if he pulled to the shoulder of the road, pulled her into his arms and kissed her until her lips softened, parted, clung to his?

He would not do it, of course; he was done with kissing her or even touching her. He wasn't interested in her anymore; it was just idle thought...

"And," she said, "I am not letting you drive one more mile until you tell me where—"

"Sicily."

Just as he'd figured, shock replaced the look of fury on her face.

"Sicily? You and I are going to—"

"Right. You and I, and a pilot."

That was when Anna saw the sign. Aeroporto Ciampino. She didn't hesitate, didn't stop to weigh her words. She simply swung toward him and said, "No!"

"In fact..." Draco checked his mirror, accelerated, swung around a black van in the lane ahead. "We're running late. I want to be off the ground before—"

"Listen to me, Draco. I am not flying anywhere with you."

"We aren't flying 'anywhere,' *consigliere,* we're flying to Sicily."

"Forget the word games! And stop calling me *consigliere.*"

"It's what you are, aren't you?"

"I am not my father's counselor. I am not even his lawyer. I'm his daughter, and I am not letting you take me to Sicily."

"Wow," Draco said, his voice thick with sarcasm, "so much information in one breath! I'm impressed."

"Damn you, Valenti—"

Anna gave a little cry as he swung the wheel hard to the right, pulled onto the shoulder of the road and put the car in neutral.

"Frankly," he said, turning toward her, his eyes, his words, cold, "I don't care what you call yourself, lady. You came to Italy to do a job for your old man. You made threats. You—"

"Threats?" Anna laughed. "What, do you think

I'm carrying a pistol? That I'm going to put a gun to your head and—"

Draco moved fast. Too fast for her to protest. One heartbeat, he was sitting next to her; the next, he'd pulled her half over the gear shift and into his arms.

"I know every inch of you," he said in a low voice. His hand swept up her side, cupped her breast; Anna gasped and tried to slap his hand away, but he wouldn't let her. "So, no, I don't think you're going to threaten me physically." His eyes grew dark and hot. "Hell," he growled, "you're already a physical threat, Anna. When you're in my arms, when you're looking at me the way you are now, *Dio,* I can't think straight."

"I don't know what you mean. And you'd better let go of me, Valenti. Let go, or—"

Draco cupped the back of her head and brought her mouth to his. Anna stiffened, tried to twist away…and then she moaned, wound her arms around his neck and sucked his tongue into her mouth.

The kiss was long and deep; it left her shaken. When Draco finally drew back, she was trembling.

"This is crazy," she whispered. "Just plain crazy! We cannot—"

"Yes," Draco said roughly, "we can."

"One minute we're enemies. The next...the next—"

He kissed her again, his lips gentle on hers, so gentle that she wanted to sigh, to melt, to stay in his arms not so much for the sexual pleasure she knew he could bring her but for the simple joy of feeling his arms around her.

The thought was unsettling, and she tore her lips from his. He let her do it, let her turn her head and lay it against his chest.

"Please." Her voice was low, almost breathless. "Please, Draco. Don't."

Draco held Anna close, one hand stroking her hair, the other on the small of her back.

He was a man who'd had considerable experience with women. Perhaps that was putting it modestly. He'd been with a lot of women, all of them willing and eager. Sometimes, despite all the talk of women meaning what they said, women who said "don't" meant just the opposite.

"Don't," a woman might say, even as she put

her hand over your fly. "Don't," she'd say, even as she moaned into your mouth and rubbed against you. "Don't," she'd whisper, when she wanted you to tell her why she should be saying "Do."

That was how he knew, with all the instincts of a man holding an aroused woman in his arms, that "don't" was not what Anna really meant.

She wanted him.

He could hear it in her voice, feel it in the way she trembled in his arms, in the way she remained curled tightly against him. One more drugging kiss. One more caress and she would whisper his name, lift her mouth to his, kiss him with all the passion he knew was in her.

But he didn't kiss her, or touch her. Instead, he went on holding her, his eyes closed, his face buried in her hair. Long moments went by before he raised his head.

"Anna."

She sighed. Then she sat up and her eyes met his.

His heart turned over.

Delicate and strong, his Anna. His beautiful, beautiful Anna.

"Anna." Draco stroked back the riot of curls that had come loose from her ponytail. "Something is happening with us, *bellissima*."

Anna shook her head.

"We're attracted to each other," she said quickly. "Why make it sound so unusual?"

She was right. There was nothing unusual in a man and a woman desiring each other. So why did her swift denial anger him?

Draco sat up straight. Checked for traffic, then pulled onto the road.

"We both want more of what happened last night," he said brusquely. "Don't waste time denying it, Anna. You know I'm speaking the truth."

Anna smoothed back her hair, redid the ponytail, folded her hands in her lap.

Damnit, why were they shaking?

"It doesn't matter," she said. "There's still the land."

"Exactly. That's why we're going to Sicily. We'll settle this thing once and for all. And then—"

"And then," Anna said firmly, "I'll go home."

* * *

The plane was a small private jet, all leather and luxury inside. The pilot and Draco shook hands, Draco introduced Anna, all of it done with the politeness of people doing business for the first time.

Not Draco's plane, then, Anna thought as she settled into her seat.

"It's a rental," Draco said as if she'd spoken the thought aloud. "Mine is en route to Rome, from Hawaii."

Rome. Hawaii. Sicily, and hadn't some of the documents in her father's file carried a San Francisco address?

The prince knew his way around the world.

Around women, too. That was why she felt so confused. It wasn't him. Or rather it was, but not because of anything special he made her feel. She was confused because he was so suave, so sophisticated, so damned smooth. She knew men who thought they were all those things, but she'd never known one like Draco.

And that was over.

She'd come to Italy on business, and this trip to Sicily wasn't going to change that.

A couple of hours from now she'd have seen

whatever earthshaking thing he wanted her to see, and then Rome and Sicily and Prince Draco Valenti would be history.

Wrong. W-r-o-n-g. Wrong, wrong, wrong.

The flight took just a little over an hour. Draco had arranged for a rental car to be waiting at Catania for the drive to Taormina. It was some kind of sturdy-looking SUV, and once they were under way, Anna understood why he'd chosen it.

Put simply, the roads.

Taormina was a tourist destination. She'd had, at least, enough time to determine that before setting off for Rome. And from what she saw of it as they drove through, it was charming. Cobbled streets, winding alleyways, the incredible blue of the Ionian Sea and, of course, the breathtakingly beautiful Mount Etna, the heat of its volcanic breath rising against a cloudless sky.

Then they left the town behind.

The road grew narrower and rougher. It twisted around mountains, clung to rocky slopes, climbed and climbed and climbed.

"I thought the Orsini land was in Taormina," Anna said as she tried to keep from clinging to the edges of her seat.

Draco looked at her.

"My land, you mean."

Anna rolled her eyes.

"Could you just answer the question? Is it in Taormina or isn't it?"

"Sure. More or less. Definitions of what is and isn't a boundary line are a little less stringent here than in Rome. Or Manhattan."

"Shouldn't we have stopped at the town hall? Or wherever it is they keep real estate records?"

"They keep records, all right. Some go back a couple of thousand years."

Anna raised an eyebrow. "Well, then—"

"My lawyers sent copies of all that stuff to your father weeks and weeks ago. Didn't you read it?"

"I did," she said, lying through her teeth. "And nothing I read changed my mind. I only meant it might be helpful to have the deed, whatever, with us right now."

Draco nodded.

"I sent your old man photos, too. Did he pass those along to you?"

Photos. Photos? Anna did a quick mental review of the material she'd seen.

"What kind of photos?"

Draco took his hand off the gearshift and held it out to her. "What do you see?"

What, indeed?

A strong, very masculine hand. Tanned skin. Long fingers. Without warning, she thought of how those fingers had felt, learning the curves of her body.

"What do you see?" he demanded.

Anna looked away.

"A hand. Am I supposed to congratulate you for having one instead of a tentacle?"

He laughed. "Nice."

"Thank you," she said primly. "I thought so."

"Look again."

"Listen, Valenti, you may find this amusing, but—"

He put his hand on her thigh. She swallowed hard. His hand was hot. So hot. She could feel its heat straight through her jeans.

"See this ring?"

Anna looked down. Yes. She saw it. The ring he wore was obviously old. Very old. It was made of gold. And it had a...

"Is that a crest?" She looked at Draco. "I never saw you wear that ring before."

He took his hand away, downshifted, took the SUV through a hairpin curve that left Anna certain they were going to fall into the sea.

"I don't wear it," Draco said, his eyes on the road, his voice low. "I'm not into jewelry. Besides, it is irreplaceable."

"Irreplaceable?"

"There hasn't been another like it for a thousand years."

Anna blinked. "A thousand…"

"*Sì.*"

She looked at the ring again. "And the crest?"

Draco cleared his throat. "The Valenti crest. The mark of my family. The mark that is on the once-crumbling pile of marble my father brought to near ruin in Rome."

"I don't understand. What has that to do with—"

He braked. Hard. The SUV jerked to a stop.

"Look," he said.

It was hard to take her eyes from Draco, but finally she did.

And caught her breath.

Ahead was a castle. Or what remained of a castle. A tower. Wide stone steps. Ancient stone walls. The ruins were stark against the blue of the sky.

Draco opened his door and stepped out of the SUV. So did Anna. He held out his hand; she hesitated. Then she took it and they walked slowly across the clearing.

"Look at the wall," he said. "Do you see what is chiseled in it? There, just above the steps."

Anna looked at the wall. Her breath caught. "It's—it's the crest."

He nodded. "The deed, if you will, and more telling than any piece of paper—though there are those, too."

A falcon called out high above them, its cry poignant and chill.

"This was once a great castle," Draco said softly. "My great-great who knows how many times great-grandfather built it. He was not like my father, or my father's father, who brought dishonor to our name. He was a man others respected, you understand? He cared for his people, defended them and this place against robbers, against barbarians, he and his sons and the sons of his sons. But eventually all things end. Invaders came from across the sea." Draco took a long breath. "The land and the castle were lost. After that, who knows? Somehow a Valenti prince put down roots in Rome. Maybe he forgot this place existed. Maybe he wanted to forget it." Draco shook his head. "I didn't know anything about the castle, the land, or the Valenti connection to Sicily until a year or so ago."

"How did you find out?"

"I was in Palermo on business. After a couple of days I felt the need to get away for a few hours. So I rented a car, took a drive...."

"And ended up here."

Draco nodded. "It was by accident, I know, but I drove around that last curve, saw this ruin...I don't know how to say it. It seemed somehow familiar. Crazy, perhaps, but I got out of the car, walked up to these steps..."

Anna traced her fingers lightly over the crest chiseled into the stone. Then she put her hand on Draco's arm. His muscles were tight as steel.

"No," she said softly, "not crazy at all." She smiled when he took his gaze from the ruins of what had surely once been a magnificent castle and looked, instead, at her. "You walked to the steps, and you saw the Valenti crest."

Draco nodded. "Yes." He shrugged as if it were not important, but the darkness in his eyes told her that it was. "I don't know if you can understand what it was like to discover that I carry the blood of brave, good men in my veins."

Could she understand? Anna wanted to laugh. Or maybe cry.

"I understand all too well," Anna said gently. "And now you're going to restore the castle."

A muscle knotted in his jaw.

"Yes. *Sì.* I am." His smile was fleeting. "Trust me, *bellissima.* My architect and builder assure me that this wish is crazy."

Was this truly Prince Draco Valenti? Did her arrogant, take-no-prisoners aristocrat actually have a heart?

Not that he was hers. Not that she would want him to be hers. There was nothing logical to that idea, nothing rational about it…

"I know succeeding in this is important to you, Anna. Securing the land for your family, I mean. But—"

To hell with logic.

Anna grasped Draco's shirt, lifted herself to him and pressed her lips to his.

CHAPTER ELEVEN

THE drive back to Catania seemed to take forever.

How could it not, when Draco kept pulling the SUV onto the shoulder of the road so he could draw Anna into his arms and kiss her?

He kept telling himself that the exquisite torture would end once they boarded the plane. Then they'd have all the privacy they needed.

He gathered her into his arms as soon as they were in the air.

She came to him with hot eagerness, straddling him, her kisses wild and abandoned, her hands on him and his on hers until he made a sound that was half groan, half laugh, leaned his forehead against hers and said, "*Bellissima.* You're killing me."

"Am I?" she whispered, and the delight in her voice made him laugh again.

"You know you are." He pressed his lips to the hollow of her throat, felt the swift race of her blood just beneath the delicate skin. "Anna. I've never wanted a woman the way I want you." He paused. "But we're going to wait." He wrapped his arms around her, gathered her tightly against him. She was trembling, *Dio,* so was he. He kissed her hair, her temple, her eyes. "We are going to wait until we are alone. Until there is all the time in the world for us."

For us. Anna closed her eyes, buried her face in his shoulder, inhaled the glorious scent of him, of his arousal.

"I want you in my bed, not on a plane, not in a hotel room." He gave a soft laugh. "It makes no sense, I know, but—but that is what I want, Anna. You and me and a quiet place that belongs only to us."

Gently he cupped the back of her head, tilted it so that their eyes met.

"I love having sex with you," he said gruffly. "But it's time to make love."

What he'd said hung between them. He hadn't planned it; he wasn't even sure what it meant. He only knew that it was true. He, the pragmatist, the man who thought *making love* was a phrase used by romantic fools, wanted to do exactly that.

Now he waited for Anna's answer. He stroked his hand the length of her back, soothing her, steadying himself. Waited for her to tell him he was wrong, that sex was sex, that she didn't want to be in his bed, to lie in his arms, that all she wanted was quick, passionate release....

"Yes," she whispered. Her lips curved in a tender smile. "Take me to your bed, Draco. And make love to me."

Something inside him took wing. "Anna," he said, *"il mio amore..."*

He kissed her. Kissed her deeply. And held her in his arms all the way to Rome.

The night was very dark, the ancient Appian Way lit only by a quarter moon and a scattering of stars that some ancient god might have tossed against the firmament.

The tall pines sighed at the caress of a warm summer breeze.

Draco led Anna through the shadow-filled silence of his villa, to his bedroom, where he turned on a lamp that shed a pale, ethereal glow over the bed.

Then he took her hands and drew her to him.

Dio, how lovely she was! Her hair streamed down her back in long, loose curls of palest gold. Her blue eyes glittered as she raised them to his. She was beautiful beyond any woman he had ever known.

Even her name was beautiful, he thought, and he spoke it now as she came into his arms.

He bent to her and kissed her.

She rose on her toes, wrapped her arms around his neck and returned kiss for kiss.

It was almost as if they had never been intimate before. He knew Anna felt it, too; she looked up at him, her lips delicately parted, her eyes luminous and filled with questions.

The questions weren't hers alone.

Last night had been incredible. Such passion. Such desire. But this—this was not the same. It was a different kind of passion, a new kind of desire. It was a storm, building inside him.

The seconds ticked away. Then Anna stepped back and reached for the hem of her T-shirt.

He caught her wrists, brought her hands to his lips, kissed each with lingering tenderness.

"I want to undress you," he said in a low voice.

A tremor went through her. "Yes," she whispered, "oh yes."

He caught hold of the bottom of the shirt, eased it up, drew her free of it and tossed it aside.

His heart turned over.

Her bra was pale peach silk, almost the color of her skin. Her breasts swelled above the delicate cups. Ripe fruit, awaiting the touch of his hands, the heat of his mouth.

Draco bent his head and pressed a kiss to each curve of lush flesh within the silken cups. Anna moaned, cupped her breasts, made them an offering to his desire and hers, but he took her hands and brought them to her sides.

Not yet. Not yet.

Her jeans rode low on her hips. He undid the button, opened the zipper, his eyes never leaving hers. He saw the color in her face deepen, heard her breathing quicken. She made a little sound, half moan, half sigh.

He was killing them both.

What an exquisite way to die.

Inch by inch, torment by torment.

There would be no mercy for her, or for him.

He was already hard as a man could be without groaning but this—this was a special kind of pain, and worth whatever it took to endure.

He would not rush this night.

He knelt. Unlaced the laces of her sneakers. Her feet were bare, the arches high and feminine. He curved his hand around one ankle, then the other, and slipped the sneakers off. Then he rose again, hooked his thumbs into the jeans and slowly, slowly eased them down her hips and legs.

Draco got to his feet, everything in him tight and intense, his eyes narrowing to dark slits as Anna stepped free of the jeans.

All she had on now were the bra and a matching thong that cupped her like the hand of a lover.

His hand, he thought. Only his.

A muscle flexed in his jaw.

She was half-naked, all hot skin and cool silk. He took one step forward, his eyes on hers, and curved his palm over the bit of silk between her thighs.

Anna cried out.

He could feel all his good intentions coming apart.

"Anna," he said, the single word hot with warning.

"Draco," she whispered, and she smiled, such a sexy smile, so wicked, so filled with the knowledge of Eve.

He knew she was remembering last night and how they'd said those same words when he'd stormed into her hotel room. He would have smiled, too, but suddenly she was touching him, her fingers at his zipper, dragging it down, and his rigid length sprang free into her hand, her fingers wrapping as best they could around his engorged flesh.

"Now," she said, and any coherent thought he might have still possessed flew from his head.

He swung her into his arms, carried her to the bed. Tore off his clothes. Came down to her and she arched toward him, seeking his mouth, her tongue a sliver of silk against his, her teeth nipping at his lip, her soft cries burning, burning into his brain.

Draco caught her wrists. Raised her arms over her head, his fingers manacles of steel.

"What do you want?" he said thickly. "Tell me."

"You," Anna said, "you, Draco, please, please, I want you. I need you…"

"Only me," he growled. "Say it, Anna."

"Yes, yes. Only you. Only you. Only—"

She screamed as he thrust into her, hard, fast, deep. Her cry filled the night; he felt her muscles contract around him.

"Open your eyes," he said roughly. "Look at me."

Her lashes rose. Her eyes wild and hot, filled with him.

"Draco," she sobbed, "Draco…"

He let go of her wrists, slid his hands beneath her, lifting her into his hard body, into the steady demand of a primitive rhythm. She moved with him, her hair flung over the pillow, her hands clutching his biceps.

He could feel the tension building in his body, in his scrotum. *Wait,* he told himself, *wait for her to come again…*

She did. Once. Twice. He heard Anna cry his name, felt her fingers dig deep into his buttocks. And then he stopped thinking, gave in to the pleasure that was more than pleasure, let it consume him.

Let it consume them both as they flew off the edge of the world into the black Roman night.

Time slipped past.

A minute. An hour. Anna couldn't tell. It didn't matter. Time had no meaning.

Only this was important.

Draco, collapsed over her, his skin as slick with sweat as hers, his heart hammering the same as hers, his breathing as ragged as hers.

Her arms were wrapped around him. One leg was draped over his hip. She had no idea where she began and he ended, and she sighed and thought she could stay like this forever.

"Too heavy," he grunted, hearing her sigh, but she shook her head, kissed his shoulder, held him even closer and that was a damned good thing because he wasn't sure that he could move.

He sure as hell didn't want to.

"Stay," she murmured, and he grunted again and let his muscles go slack.

After another minute, or maybe another hour, he said something.

"Mmm," Anna said, because she had no idea

what it was but she figured that *mmm* would cover all possibilities.

He laughed and rolled onto his side, taking her with him.

"'Mmm' what?"

"Mmm to whatever you asked me," she said lazily.

Draco nuzzled a spill of curls off her cheek. "I didn't ask. I said."

Her lips curved in a lazy smile. "The authoritative prince."

"Damned right." He rolled again, this time onto his back, taking her with him so that she lay sprawled over him like a blanket. *A warm, silken blanket,* he thought, his arms tight around her.

"I said so much for the best-laid plans."

"I am," Anna said primly, "very well laid, Your Highness, and thank you for asking."

Draco laughed. "I'm happy to hear it."

"So what were these plans?" she said, and kissed his shoulder.

"I was going to make love to you very, very slowly," he said, running his hand up and down the length of her spine.

"Ah. *Those* plans." She lifted her head, folded

her hands on his chest, propped her chin on them and smiled. "You looking for compliments, Valenti? 'Cause if you are, all things considered, I think we did pretty well."

There it was again, that wickedly sexy smile. Combined with the feel of her draped over him, it was causing trouble with his anatomy.

"You do, huh?"

"Ladies and gentlemen of the jury," she said in her best courtroom voice, "consider the evidence."

He shifted, just a little. "What evidence?"

"The evidence," Anna said. "You know. Exhibit A. And exhibit—" Her breath caught as he shifted again. "Exhibit B," she whispered. "Definitely exhibit—"

He cupped one hand around the nape of her neck and brought her mouth to his. His kiss was sweet and tender; she could feel a honeyed warmth spreading through her body.

No, she thought as his kiss deepened. Not just through her body. The warmth was everywhere. In her lips, as they clung to his.

And in her heart.

The realization made her tremble. Draco rolled her beneath him.

"Anna. What is it, *bellissima?*"

"Draco," she whispered, and his lips found hers, moved over hers with passion and tenderness. "Draco," she said again, and then she wound her arms tightly around her lover's neck, and the world, and reality, fell away.

Sometime between midnight and dawn, long after the moon had set, Anna awoke to Draco's kisses.

"Mmm," she said sleepily, and he smiled and brushed his lips lightly over hers.

"Such an extensive vocabulary, *il mio amore,*" he said softly. "I'm glad we agree."

Anna yawned. "Mmm," she said again, and started to snuggle deeper into his arms.

"Anna. Surely those *mmm*s meant 'Yes, Draco. I agree. I'm starving. I can't even remember the last time we had anything to eat.'"

Anna blinked her eyes open. "You're right. I can't."

"Exactly. We need food. Sustenance. That

which gives a man energy to survive the difficult demands put on him by a woman."

That made her laugh. "Such a sacrifice, Valenti."

Draco caught her bottom lip in his teeth, nibbled gently, then ran the tip of his tongue over the sweet wound.

"What would you like?"

Anna toyed with a dark strand of hair that had fallen over his forehead.

"A Big Mac and fries?"

He grinned. "How about some pasta? Tomato sauce. Black olives. Garlic. Anchovies. Freshly grated Romano cheese. And whatever else is in the refrigerator." He raised one eyebrow. "How does that sound?"

"Like takeout from this amazing little Italian place down the block from my office. One problem, though. In case you hadn't noticed, we're a few thousand miles from Manhattan."

Draco tossed back the duvet and sat up.

"I," he said smugly, "just happen to be a world-class cook!"

She sat up, too, and gave him a look. "You, Valenti?"

"Me, *consigliere,*" he said as he strode into what Anna assumed was a dressing room.

He was, she thought, a gorgeous man. All hard muscle, taut definition and potent masculinity.

But he was more than that.

So much more.

Charming. Strong. Determined. Opinionated. Arrogant. Tender. Sweet.

He was all those things, some of them total contradictions, and how could that be? How could he be so many different things to her?

He was—he was wonderful. Being with him was wonderful, not only in bed but in so many ways.

She loved talking with him. She loved joking with him. She loved being held in his arms.

She loved—she loved—

"Anna?"

Anna blinked. Draco was back, wearing sweatpants, holding open a deep blue terry-cloth robe.

She stared at him. Her heart was beating fast. No. The idea was insane. You didn't fall in love with a man in, what, forty-eight hours. She certainly didn't. She didn't fall in love at all!

She didn't even know what love was...or maybe

she did. Yes, damned right, she did. Love was a trap. It was the way nature reminded you that you were a second-class citizen, that once you gave yourself up to a man, you were whatever he wanted you to be and not what you'd wanted to be.

"*Bellissima?* Why such a shocked look on that beautiful face?"

She took a deep breath.

"Nothing. Well, I mean—I mean, it's terribly late. I—I should get back to the hotel."

"Anna." He came toward her slowly, his eyes locked to hers. "What are you talking about?"

"The time. How late it is. And—"

"I don't want you to leave."

Anna grabbed the robe from his hands, stood up and quickly slipped it on. She didn't want to be naked. As it was, she felt—she felt totally, terrifyingly exposed.

"Well, but it isn't up to you, is it?" Her voice was brittle. She hated the sound, hated the way he was looking at her, the way she felt, confused and desperate, and there was this unpleasant, leaden feeling in her heart... "It's up to me if I want to leave, and—"

She gasped as Draco pulled her into his arms. "I would not have thought the Orsini *consigliere* would be a coward."

"I'm not a coward. And I told you, I'm not a *consigliere*. I hate my father and what he stands for, and the only *famiglia* I'm part of is the one made up of my four brothers and my sister, and if you don't let go of me, Draco Valenti, I'll— I'll—"

Draco muttered a rough phrase in Italian, hauled her to her toes and kissed her. Anna fought the kiss.

No. Not the kiss. She fought what she felt, the floodgate of emotion opening in her heart.

She trembled as Draco took his lips from hers and drew her close.

"*Lo so, tesoro,*" he whispered. "I know. You don't understand this. Neither do I." He stroked her hair, pressed his lips to her temple. "Something different, *sì?* This—this feeling. This emotion..."

She gave a watery laugh.

"Pasta and philosophy. What more could one ask for in the middle of the night?"

He laughed, too, and gathered her to him.

She could feel his heart beating. He could feel hers.

They stood that way for a long time. Then Anna leaned back in her lover's arms.

"Draco," she said softly.

"Anna," he said just as softly.

They smiled, both thinking, again, of that first night together and how he had said her name and she had said his.

He cupped her face. Kissed her so tenderly she felt tears in her eyes.

After a long time he stepped back. Tied the sash of the robe at her waist. Looked at her, from the tips of her bare toes to the top of her tousled curls.

His smile lit her heart.

"Sei cosi bella," he said softly.

He took her hand and kissed it. Then, fingers entwined, he led her through the still-dark villa to the kitchen.

CHAPTER TWELVE

DRACO had told the truth.

Almost.

He wasn't a world-class chef, but he made world-class espresso. Anna pronounced it amazing as they sat drinking it at a small marble-topped table in the garden just off the kitchen.

"Not even my mother makes better coffee," she told him.

"That," he said solemnly, "has to be a world-class compliment."

She grinned. "You'd better believe it."

The sun was rising, shedding streaks of gold through the garden and the pines that surrounded it.

Anna sighed. "It's lovely here," she said softly. "The only thing missing is music."

"The Pines of Rome," Draco said.

Anna looked at him over her coffee cup. "Yes, exactly." She smiled. "And here I thought I was the only person in the world who loved Respighi."

"Got to admit," Draco said solemnly, "for me, it's a toss-up between Respighi and Mick Jagger."

She laughed. He loved to watch her laugh. There was nothing delicate or false about it, the way there was with so many women.

"Well, heck," she said, "why not? I mean, they're both golden oldies."

Draco grinned. And then, because it seemed the most natural thing in the world, he leaned across the table and kissed her.

"Nice," he said. He kissed her again. Her lips parted, clung gently to his. "Very nice. The best possible way to get sugar with my espresso."

Anna's lips curved against his. "Flattery will get you everywhere. But I guess you know that, huh?"

"Me?" Draco said, with such innocence that she giggled.

He grinned, tugged her from her chair and drew her into his lap. They kissed again. And again. His hand slipped inside her robe. She moaned as he caressed her breast, and then she grabbed his hand and clasped it firmly in both of hers.

"We need food, remember?" she said sternly. "Sustenance, Valenti. You said so yourself." She got to her feet. He rose, too, collected their cups and followed her into the kitchen, where an enormous pot of sauce simmered on the stove.

It had turned out that he was not only a world-class maker of coffee, he was also a world-class slicer and dicer of onions, garlic, celery, tomatoes—all the stuff they'd pilfered from the fridge and pantry and combined in a pot.

It had been simmering for an hour. Now Draco took a deep, deep breath.

"Wow."

Anna nodded. "Wow, indeed."

"It smells wonderful."

"That's 'cause I'm the chef," she said smugly, plucking a big wooden spoon from the top of the stove and stirring the sauce. "Maybe not world class, but my-mother's-kitchen class, anyway."

"Hey," he said, "we're both Italian. *Ragù* is in our genes."

"*Ragù,* as in the brand of gravy in a jar?"

"*Ragù,* as in that's the word for... Gravy? What gravy?"

Anna laughed. "If you grow up in Little Italy, this red stuff is gravy."

"Ah." Draco took the spoon and stirred the simmering sauce.

"Ah, what?"

"Nothing. I just—oof! Darn it, woman, that is a very sharp elbow."

"Did you just make a disparaging comment about my ancestry?"

He gave her a look of abject innocence.

"Would I say anything disparaging about a woman who can make a pasta sauce this good? Here," he said, holding out the spoon. "Take a taste."

"From that spoon straight to my hips."

"Your hips are perfect."

"Liar," she said, trying not to smile.

"They're curvy. Feminine. Sexy. In other words, perfect. Now, come on, lady lawyer. Taste."

Anna rolled her eyes. "That is so-o-o sexist."

"Stop complaining and taste the... What did you call it? Taste the gravy."

Smiling, she leaned toward him. Draco whisked the spoon away and captured her mouth with his.

"Mmm," he said softly.

"Mmm, indeed."

Draco swept his arms around her. "*Mmm* is becoming my favorite word."

She reached up and brushed a dark lock of hair off his forehead. "Mine, too."

"In that case…"

He kissed her again. And again.

Anna laid her hand against his jaw, felt the roughness of early-morning stubble beneath the tips of her fingers. So sexy. So masculine. It felt that way, too. Against her hand. And, God, against her breasts. Her belly. Her thighs.

Had she really thought she didn't like that sensation? That, and coming awake in a man's arms. Why had that always seemed as if it would surely be something to avoid?

Turned out it wasn't.

In fact, there were definite benefits.

Morning sex. Something she'd never thought was all that movies and books made it out to be. But it was. It was lovely. Absolutely lovely when the man was Draco.

"Such deep, deep thoughts, *bellissima*."

She blinked. Draco was watching her with the kind of all-or-nothing intensity that was one of the first things she'd noticed about him.

Liked about him.

Liked very much. Very, very much…

"Anna." He set the spoon aside, gathered her into his arms. "What is it, *cara?*"

She swallowed hard, worked up a smile.

"I was just thinking that this is the first time, the very first time in my life, I'm going to have pasta for breakfast."

Draco watched as she busied herself with the *ragù.* He took the pot he assumed his housekeeper used for pasta from a cupboard, brought it to the sink and filled it with water.

Was that really what she'd been thinking? Pasta for breakfast? A first for him, too…

There were more firsts for him this morning than pasta.

Early-morning conversation with a woman. Breakfast with her. No thought at all of business. That alone was inconceivable, that he should have awakened as he had, his thoughts not on the day's business agenda or how the New York market would open but on, of all things, a woman.

And what, exactly, did that mean?

The water began to boil.

Draco lowered the flame and wished he could

lower the boiling point of whatever it was that was happening inside him.

A muscle knotted in his jaw.

Anna was still at the stove, concentrating on stirring the sauce as if her life depended on it.

Was she as confused as he was?

Yesterday he'd told her that something was happening. The question was, what? He needed time and space to clear his head.

"Draco."

He looked at Anna. Her face was pale.

"I have to leave."

He didn't answer.

"Go back to New York, I mean."

Still he didn't respond. Anna expelled a breath.

"I came to do a job and I've done it." She gave a little laugh. "I mean, I came to do a job and now I know there's no job to do. The land is absolutely yours. I don't even know how my father came up with that story, but—"

"I understand," he said politely…and then he looked at her, really looked at her, and felt himself growing angry. At her. At him. At them both. He moved toward her, clasped her shoulders, pulled her to her toes and glowered. "Goddamnit, Anna, you're not going anywhere!"

"Don't be ridiculous. I have to."

"What you have to do is stay here. With me."

"No." Her voice took on a panicked edge. "I can't. My work—"

"I have work, too. Call your office, as I will call mine. Tell them you won't be in for a week."

"Draco. I can't simp—"

He kissed her. Again and again, his arms hard around her, until she was hanging on to him to keep her knees from buckling.

"Stop," she whispered. "I can't think when you—"

"I am not asking you to think. I am asking you to do."

Oh, he was so sure of himself! So arrogant. So demanding. So certain that because he was a man, he could bend her to his will.

"I have a job," she said. "A life. I have commitments…"

Dark fire flashed in his eyes. "To a man?"

"No! Never. See? You don't know anything about me or you'd never have asked me a thing like—"

"What I know," he said, "is that we aren't done with this."

"Done with what?" Anna gathered herself together. "Look. It's been—it's been—"

"Sì," he said in a low voice, "it has. But it isn't over." He let go of her, reached for the phone, held it out. "Call your office. Call whoever needs to be called. Tell them you'll be gone a week."

Anna looked at her lover. At the phone in his outstretched hand. *Arrogant* wasn't the word to describe him. It didn't even come close. No one had told her what to do since she'd turned eighteen. Hell, she'd stopped listening to those who'd tried long before that.

And now this man, this impossible, tough-and-tender man thought he could step into her life with orders and demands?

"Anna." Draco kissed her. Gently. Tenderly. *"Per favore, mio amore,"* he said softly. "I beg you. Stay with me this week."

Anna stared into his eyes. Took a deep breath. Took the telephone from him.

And made the call.

* * *

They ate bowls of delicious pasta. Showered. Then Draco said he wanted to show her his Rome.

"I hate to say it," he told her, "but it's time to get dressed."

Dressed in what?

Anna groaned as she looked at the clothes she'd left on a chair in his bedroom. "Oh no," she whispered.

Draco, who was zipping up a pair of chino trousers, looked at her.

"What's wrong, *cara?*"

"If there's anything worse than wearing the same stuff two days in a row—"

"Ah," he said. "That."

"Yes. That. I don't even have a change of underwear."

"But you do."

"I do?"

His smile was as smug as any she'd ever seen.

"*Sì.* Your clothes, your makeup—although why you'd put gunk on such a beautiful face is beyond me—all of that is here."

Anna stared at him. "Here?"

"Of course. I took care of it."

"You took—"

"Anna," Draco said gently, "stop repeating what I say. Yes, I took care of it. I arranged for the hotel to pack for you and my driver to bring your luggage here. My housekeeper put everything in the dressing room. Didn't you notice?"

"Well, no. But then, I didn't expect…" She paused. "Let me get this straight. You made all these arrangements without asking me?"

Draco slipped on a white cotton shirt, did up most of the buttons, then folded back the sleeves.

"What was there to ask? I knew you would want your belongings."

"Did you also know I'd be amenable to staying here instead of at my hotel?"

"Amenable. Lady lawyer talk," he said, smiling as he reached for her.

Anna stepped back. "Don't do that."

"Don't do what?"

"Don't try and—and make fun of what I say."

"Whoa." Draco held up his hands. "All I did was—"

"This may surprise you, but I can think for myself."

His smile fled. "Such a mistake," he said stiffly. "A man tries to do a good thing for his woman—"

"I am not your woman. I am not anyone's woman. I am my own…" Anna caught her lip between her teeth. *His woman.* She had to admit there was something special in the words. "Hell," she said softly. "I'm behaving like a fool."

Draco hesitated. Then he sighed and reached for her.

"Yes," he said, "you are."

She gave a little laugh. "Thanks for agreeing with me. I think."

Smiling, he put a finger under her chin and tilted her face to his.

"Let me spoil you a little, *bellissima,* okay?"

"I'm just not used to…" She sighed. "It was very sweet of you to do what you did."

His answering grin was all sexy male arrogance.

"Yes," he said, and brushed his lips over hers. "It was."

Anna laughed as he drew her close. Learning to let a man spoil you, especially a man like Draco Valenti, was going to be a challenge.

He said there were five places you had to visit if you wanted to say you had seen Rome.

The Coliseum. The Forum. The Piazza Navona. The Trevi Fountain. And the Spanish Steps.

Today, he said, they would see the Spanish Steps.

Another of his self-assured pronouncements. This time Anna fought her instinctive—and foolish—reaction. Why should he consult her on something so simple? This was Rome, he was Roman, she wasn't. End of argument.

Besides, the Spanish Steps sounded perfect, and they were.

The stone steps, worn smooth in places by the tread of feet over hundreds of years, climbed from the beautiful Piazza di Spagna to the Piazza Trinità dei Monti. Tourists as well as Romans climbed the steps, stood on them and sat on them, enjoying the sights, the sounds, the balmy weather....

And cups and cones of cold, creamy *gelato*.

Draco took Anna to his favorite *gelateria*.

"So many flavors," she said, looking at the endless list, but it turned out she didn't have to make a choice. He ordered for them both, no questions asked. One chocolate, one *marrone*. The two best flavors, he said with his arm around her, keeping her close to his side.

What about lemon? she almost said, but didn't. The day was perfect. So was the man. The truth was, there was something sexy to this me-Tarzan, you-Jane approach that she had so recently laughed at.

As long as it didn't go too far.

They found places to sit on the steps, one right above the other. Draco took the upper step; Anna took the one beneath it and leaned back against his legs.

She took a long lick of chocolate *gelato.* Draco's eyes followed the motion of her tongue.

"Now try the *marrone,*" he said softly.

She licked at the chestnut ice cream, caught an almost-spilled drop at the corner of her mouth with the tip of her tongue.

"You," Draco said in a low voice, "are asking for trouble."

She looked up at him. "What kind of trouble?" she said with a teasing smile, and he laughed and deposited a quick, ice-cream-sweet kiss on her lips.

Anna sat back again, Draco at her back, the Roman sun on her face, the *gelato* cool in her mouth. *Wonderful,* she thought. All of it. The city. The piazza. The *gelato.*

The man.

Most especially the man.

He was so different from what she'd expected, so different from the men she usually dated. He was beautiful to look at, yes, but what made him unique was harder to pin down, that tantalizing combination of strength and tenderness, that old-fashioned belief in honor…

That male arrogance.

Back to that again.

She'd always hated it.

Well, no.

She hated it in her father, where arrogance equated with dominance. In the men who sur-rounded him. She hated it in a handful of her colleagues, who sometimes spoke to her as if she were a girl and not a woman.

But her brothers were male to the core; they were incredibly arrogant and yet she loved that in them—their assertiveness, their protectiveness…

Her sisters-in-law, independent females every one, clearly loved those same qualities. Maybe whether you thought a man's attitude was caring or dominating depended on what you felt for the man. On whether you respected him and admired him.

On whether you loved him—whatever that meant, because she didn't believe in love. In the very concept of it. In being with one man forever, waking up in his arms, falling asleep with your hand on his heart, feeling peace inside you just because you did something simple like—like sitting in the sun, eating ice cream while you leaned against him...

The cup of *gelato* slipped from her hand.

"Such a waste," Draco teased as he scooped it up. Then he saw her face. "Anna? What is it?"

What, indeed? It wasn't possible. It absolutely wasn't. She was—she was a victim of her own imagination. The beautiful city. The beautiful man. A hundred movies and magazine articles with Rome as the setting, and that was all it was, this—this sudden gallop of her heart.

"Anna. Answer me. Are you ill?"

"No. No! I'm fine."

Draco rose and drew her to her feet. "Are you sure?" His eyes were dark with worry.

"I'm positive. Too much sun maybe." She managed a smile. "Or maybe too much ice cream after too much pasta. I mean, when your usual breakfast is whole wheat toast..."

He was supposed to laugh. Instead, he drew her into his arms.

"I know exactly what you need."

There it was again. That damnable male attitude. No. She could never—

"In fact," he said, his voice a rough caress meant for her ears alone, "I know precisely what you need. A cool drink. A cool bed. And my arms, warm around you."

He was right.

He was right, and whatever that meant was...

It was terrifying.

Over the next few days Draco showed Anna more of his Rome.

The ancient, narrow streets. The magnificent fountains. The green parks. The centuries worth of paintings and frescoes and sculptures. The passageways beneath the Coliseum, where she could almost hear the cries, smell the fear of the men and the animals about to die in the arena.

And he wanted to buy her things. A carnival

mask from Venice. A tiny bejeweled heart from Bulgari. Each time, she offered a polite "Thank you, but no."

He tried to overrule that *no* in a tiny, elegant shop on the Via Condotti, where he'd taken her after she said she really, really needed to buy some clothes, emphasis on the *really, really* in a way that told him what he already suspected—that his Anna wasn't accustomed to spending much on herself.

Except for shoes. "My weakness," she'd admitted one night, and he told her he was glad that it was, because the sight of her long, lovely legs in those killer heels, the rest of her clad only in a thong and matching bra, was fast becoming his.

But when she said she needed to get something to wear, that she couldn't live in her lady lawyer suits, one pair of jeans and that T-shirt that made him laugh each time he saw it, Draco took her to the only place he could think of. The Via Condotti, its endless designer shops…

A mistake.

Any of the women who'd passed through his life would have been thrilled.

Anna was horrified.

"Ohmygod, look at the prices!" she'd hissed—at least she'd hissed it when there were prices to see. There were no tags on the things in some shops; when Anna asked, the clerk would ignore her and give the answer to him.

That they would assume he'd pay for her purchases made Anna even more indignant.

"Anna," he'd said softly, "*bellissima,* be reasonable. This is how things are done."

"Not by me."

"But I want to buy these things for you. That dress. This skirt." He picked up a tiny gold-and-Murano-glass replica of the Trevi Fountain. "And this. Imagine how it would look on your fireplace mantel. Or the desk in your office."

Imagine how it would remind you of this week we spent together, he'd meant, but it was pointless.

"That little figure," she'd said, "costs a king's ransom. Besides, I don't have a fireplace or a mantel in my walk-up, and if I put it anywhere in the hole-in-the-wall I call an office, one of my scruffy clients would try and steal it."

A walk-up flat. A miserable office. Clients who probably spent more time making excuses for their failures than doing something about them. She deserved better than that, but he'd known that telling her so was pointless.

Almost as pointless as their shopping expedition until a clerk had taken pity on her, or maybe on him, and whispered the name of a place blocks away that dealt, she said, in things far less expensive. Anna had dragged him there and left him outside to cool his heels.

When she'd emerged a quarter of an hour later, carrying a huge, plain shopping bag, he'd been surprised.

"So fast?" he'd said.

"I don't need to waste time. I know what I want when I see it."

Yes. So did he. And what he wanted was Anna.

He wanted her all the time, and she wanted him with the same hot desire. And yet the more they made love, the more he felt that heat changing to something else. Something deeper and stronger, something powerful...

And frightening.

It was on his mind all the time.

That he felt something he couldn't comprehend, and that their time together was coming to a close. Only another two days, he found himself thinking one night as they were finishing dinner on the terrace of a small, very quiet, well—off-the-tourist-route restaurant in Trastevere.

Anna was talking. Animatedly.

Draco was listening. More or less. Mostly he was filling his eyes with her.

"…haven't listened to a word," she said suddenly, and he blinked and said, "What?"

She made a face. "See? And here I was telling you all my secrets."

He reached for her hand. "I know all your secrets," he said softly. "That place on your neck that drives you crazy when I kiss it. The taste of your nipples on my tongue…"

"Stop that," she said, but her eyes glittered and her lips curved in a smile. "I'm talking about a different kind of secret. About my hair."

He looked at her hair, hanging down her back like curls of spun gold.

"I love your hair," he said.

"Yeah?" She flashed a smile so smug it made him raise his eyebrows. "I bet you wouldn't have loved it when I dyed it black."

He blinked. "You what?"

"I dyed it. Not just black. Jet-black. So then, of course, I went the whole route. Black nail polish, black lipstick, black T-shirts, black jeans…"

He tried to imagine it. And shuddered. "Why?"

"Teenage rebellion, maybe. I was, I don't know, sixteen, seventeen. Or maybe it was a way to tell my father what he could do with his version of 'young ladies are expected to be quiet, demure and obedient' nonsense."

"Was that what he expected of you?"

"Of course." Anna eyed the tray of tiny pastries that the waiter had brought with their coffee, reached for one, pulled her hand back, reached for another, did the same thing, finally sighed and gave the tray a delicate push away from her. "He had as much chance of me falling into line as a snowball has of making it through hell."

Draco smiled. *Dio,* his Anna was tough!

"And your father said…?"

"He said if this were the fifteenth century instead of the twenty-first, he'd have locked me away in a nunnery."

"I'm starting to understand that T-shirt of yours," Draco said, and grinned. "The fish and the bicycle thing. I'm just trying not to take it personally." Anna smiled. He reached for her hand and enfolded it in his. "So what did he do?"

"Well, what *could* he do?"

"Ah. No nunneries. I forgot."

"He cut off my allowance. Big deal. My brothers made up for it."

"Your brothers liked your black hair?"

"They liked that I'd stood up to our father, the way they had. Plus, I'm pretty sure they thought my Goth phase was cool. See, they're pretty cool themselves." She reached for the tray again. This time she grabbed a pastry and ate it in two quick bites. "They never took a penny from our father," she said after she'd swallowed. "And now they run this humongous investment firm in Manhattan."

Draco slapped his forehead. "Of course! Orsini Brothers."

"Uh-huh."

He chuckled. "It's perfect. A crime boss rendered powerless in his own home. Nice work, *bellissima.*"

Anna's smile broadened. "Thank you, Your Highness."

Draco brought her hand to his lips and kissed it. "Did your sister rebel, too?"

"In the most innocent-seeming way. Izzy took to digging in the soil. Getting her hands dirty. Father found that to be beneath one of his daughters. The more he objected, the more she dug." Anna's eyes danced. "Checkmate."

"Indeed."

"Okay. It's your turn."

"At what?"

"You know all about me, but I don't know a thing about you. What were you like as a kid?"

Draco's smile faded. "I was not—what did you call it? I was not cool, Anna."

Her smile faded, too. "Draco," she said softly, "I'm sorry. I should have realized. It must have been hard. Your father, your grandfather, whatever they'd done to lose everything…"

Had he told her about that? Yes. He had. What for? He didn't talk about his childhood, his family… Except that now, without planning to, he found himself talking about all of it.

About his mother, who'd never been a mother to him at all. About his father, who had, literally, never noticed if he was there or not. About boarding school, and what it had taken to survive it…

Finally he ran out of words.

He fell silent. So did Anna. He couldn't read her face at all.

"Well," he said after a minute, trying for a laugh he couldn't quite muster, "so much for ruining the evening."

Anna shoved back her chair. A second later she was crouched beside him, her eyes suspiciously bright.

Draco looked around. A score of interested people looked back.

"Damnit, Anna," he said.

"Damnit, Draco," she replied, her voice as soft as the petals of a flower, and right there, on the crowded terrace of a crowded restaurant, she clasped his face with her hands, brought it down to hers and put her lips against his.

That was the moment he knew he could not possibly let her leave him at the end of the week.

He lay awake that night long after she fell asleep.

Two more days. Then Anna would fly to New York. She had a return ticket, she'd said when he'd suggested she use his plane, which was finally back in service. He'd argued, then given in. She was so damned stubborn, too stubborn even to agree to something when anyone could see that doing so would make sense.

As for him, he'd stay on in Rome for a few days, take care of some business. Then he'd fly to San Francisco. And the week they'd spent together, their affair, if you could call seven nights and two days an affair, would be history.

They would still see each other, of course. He'd fly east, she'd fly west. A weekend here, a weekend there. It was doable.

For a while.

Well, so what?

These relationships never lasted. Hell, why would he want them to? The sex lost its excitement. Conversation lost its luster. Yes, this week had been different. Morning conversation. Late-night kisses. Things he'd never even considered with other women had become not just enjoyable but important.

Damnit. He was not ready to let Anna walk out of his life.

New York. San Francisco. Three thousand

miles. If only his offices were on the East Coast, or hers on the West. He could not change that. He'd spent years building his company. Hundreds of people worked for him. Anna, on the other hand…

Wait a minute.

What had she said about her work? A hole-in-the-wall office. Sleazy clients. A walk-up flat.

What if she had another opportunity? A much better one? She would, of course, accept it…

And just that quickly, Draco knew what to do. And how to do it so it wouldn't make her hackles rise. Underhanded? No. Clever, that was all. Clever and logical.

Carefully he eased his arm from her. "Mmm." She sighed, and he smiled, thinking of how now he'd be sure to hear that soft whisper again.

He rose, pulled on his discarded trousers and went through the villa to his study. It took a while to make the necessary phone calls. Two hours, to be precise.

And then the deed was done.

No more East-Coast, West-Coast conundrum. One coast was all they'd need.

A few days from now, Anna would be head-hunted by Vernon, Bolton and Andover, a top-flight San Francisco law firm. The firm he used, as a matter of fact. They'd explain that they'd decided to expand their *pro bono* cases and they needed an experienced litigator. They'd offer her four times her current salary, a staff and all the indigent cases they believed had merit.

And, as was often the case, the partner who recruited her would tell her they'd already scouted out an apartment she'd surely like.

By happy coincidence, it would be in the same building as Draco's condo.

Draco had given that lots of thought. He really wanted her living with him, but maybe he wasn't ready for that. Besides, he knew his Anna.

She liked feeling independent.

Having her own place, even if she spent most of her time in his, would make her happy. He'd let her pay the rent—she would believe the owner was renting it out—and Draco wouldn't be fool enough to suggest letting him pay it. But she didn't have to know that he was the owner, and that she was paying only half the actual monthly cost.

Even with her new income, she'd never be able

to afford the flat otherwise, and no way was he going to give her any excuse not to be with him.

A tiny kernel of doubt crept in.

What if it turned out she hated California? What if she didn't want to leave her family?

What if she didn't want to spend her life with him?

Well, not forever, of course. Nothing lasted forever. Still...

Still, maybe some things did. Maybe what he really wanted of her was more than a move to the West Coast. Maybe this wasn't simply about wanting her, but was about needing her. About—about—

Dio, his head was spinning.

Draco ran his hands through his hair until it stood up in unruly little peaks.

Had he acted too impulsively? He couldn't think.

He needed coffee. Or brandy. Grappa. Yes. Excellent. Some good, strong grappa so he could think through this whole thing again.

He walked quickly through the silent house, grabbed the bottle of grappa from the bar in the living room. The phone rang as he was pouring the fiery liquid, but he didn't bother answering it. What for? He knew what it was. A fax from his lawyer, confirming everything they'd arranged: Anna's new job, her new flat, the reduced monthly costs she'd never know about.

He drank off half the grappa.

He'd done the right thing. Surely he had...

Hell.

He had done a stupid thing!

How could he have woven such a lie? You didn't lie to the woman you loved, and he loved Anna. He didn't want her to be his mistress, to be at his beck and call. He wanted to be with her always, for the rest of his life. He wanted—

Something hit him, hard, in the center of his back.

Draco swung around, the grappa flying from his hand...and saw the beautiful, furious face of the woman he loved. She'd slugged him with her fist. A fist that held what were, quite obviously, the pages of a fax.

"Anna. Anna, I know what you must be thinking—"

"You—you son of a bitch!"

"Per favore, bellissima..."

"Do not," she snarled, "do not *bellissima* me, you bastard!"

"Anna. Listen to me."

"Was this the plan all along? To tell me lies and lure me to California after I passed the—the tryout for the part of your new mistress?"

"Look, I know how this must seem. But—"

"Did you or did you not arrange for me to get a new job and a new apartment?"

How had it all come apart this quickly?

"Answer me, damn you!"

"Yes," Draco said, "but—"

"How could you be so stupid? How could you even dream I would ever be any man's mistress? Especially yours!"

"I made a mistake. I know that. I didn't think. I was so—so intent on not losing you—"

"On owning me, you mean." Her voice broke. "What an idiot I was! How I could have let myself think that you—that I…"

She spun away and ran from the room, Draco on her heels, but she reached the bedroom first, slammed and locked the door.

"Anna!"

Draco pounded on the door, but it remained

closed until she flung it open. She was fully dressed: sneakers, jeans, the to-hell-with-men T-shirt, the carry-on over her shoulder, the bulging briefcase under her arm.

"I phoned for a taxi. Make sure the gate opens for it."

"Anna—"

"Damnit, Draco, did you hear what I said?"

"Anna. I beg you—"

"It was a great week," she said, her eyes, her voice, everything about her as icy and unyielding as when they'd first met. "I've never had an Italian lover before. Thanks for giving me the chance to add you to my list."

It was a solid metaphorical blow, delivered by a tough street fighter.

He had to admire her for it, even though she had just broken his heart.

CHAPTER THIRTEEN

"So, what do you think, Iz? Too much color? Not enough? What?"

Isabella Orsini stood in the center of her sister's minuscule living room, arms folded, brow furrowed, watching as Anna held paint samples against the wall.

"What I think is, it's Friday night. You want to go to a movie?"

"Answer the question. Too bright? Too dull? Which?"

Isabella sighed. "Try that orange one again."

"Which orange one? Pumpkin Patch? Russet Red? Autumn Peach?"

"That's ridiculous. Peaches are a summer fruit. There are no peaches in autumn."

"Go over to the Whole Foods on Union Square. I'll bet they have peaches."

"For goodness sake, Anna, you know what I mean."

"Just answer the question, okay? Pumpkin? Russet? Autumn?"

Isabella sighed. "You want the truth, I don't like any of them. Tell me again why we're going to paint this room?"

"So it looks different, that's why. To shake things up, that's why. Must there be a logical reason for everything?"

"Just listen to you, lady lawyer. Since when aren't you a stickler for logic?"

"Change is logical. And what's with calling me lady lawyer?"

"I don't know. I just did, that's all."

"Well, don't do it again." Anna edged out from behind the sagging sofa she'd picked up at a Bowery consignment shop the prior weekend. "Ugh! Why did I buy this gross-looking thing?"

"I have no idea. I mean, it sags. It tilts. And baby-poo brown isn't one of my favorite colors."

"Thank you. That really makes me feel better."

"Hey, you asked. Here's an idea. You take one end, I'll take the other, we'll drag it downstairs, put it at the curb—"

"We'd never move it. It weighs a ton. I had to pay the super fifty bucks to get it up here."

"And it cost you how much?"

Anna sighed. "Fifty bucks."

"So a hundred dollars for a pile of sagging baby poo when you already had a perfectly acceptable sofa?"

"It was ugly."

"Not like this." The sisters sank down on opposite ends of the offending piece of furniture and looked at each other. Isabella cleared her throat. "So, you gonna tell me what's happening?"

"You know what's happening. I have an interesting new client."

"Excellent way to describe a nut who shot out all the windows in his ex's apartment so he wouldn't have to see her and her new boyfriend through them." Izzy snorted. "Anybody break the news to him yet? That, hello, you can see through windows even better when the glass is gone?"

"And," Anna said, choosing to ignore the remark, "in addition to an interesting new client, I have a new sofa. New for me, okay? This time tomorrow I'll also have new paint on the walls. And let's not forget the boots I bought last week."

"Right. Not boots. Snow boots. And it's still summer."

"It's the end of summer. That's why they were on sale."

"Uh-huh. Maybe they were on sale 'cause only my sister would be crazy enough to buy snow boots with five-inch heels."

"Four-inch, and what's so bad with me trying to make some changes in my life?"

"Nothing," Isabelle said, "if you weren't doing it to try and bury something you don't want to think about."

Anna snorted. "That's crazy."

"That's accurate. Remember you asked me about psych 101? About sexual fantasies?"

"Isabella. I have no intention of—"

"There was more to psych 101 than that. For instance, chapter twelve of that oversize textbook, remember? Ahem. 'A sudden flurry of change-centered activity is often symptomatic of a desire to obliterate memory of a distressing situation.'"

Anna stared at her sister. "You can remember reading that?"

Iz shrugged. "Heck, no. I just made it up. But see, I'm right. I can tell. Just look at your face."

"Coffee," Anna said briskly. She sprang to her

feet and walked the six feet it took to reach the kitchen. "Get out the cream, would you? And the pink stuff."

"Anna. You went to Italy. 'I'll be gone a couple of days,' you said. Instead, you were gone a week. And when you got back, you looked like crap."

"Baby poo. Now crap. What a fine sense for similes my sister has." Anna's words were brisk, but her hands trembled as she filled the coffeepot with water. "Want some cookies?"

"I want some answers. What happened in Rome?"

"Nothing," Anna said. "Nothing at all. I saw the Trevi Fountain, the Coliseum, I did a little shopping and—"

"And?" Isabella said, narrowing her hazel eyes.

"And," Anna said, turning her back to her sister, "and…"

"Anna. Honey, you can tell me anything. You know that."

Anna nodded. She could. And, really, she had to. She couldn't carry this around inside her anymore.

"And," she said in a low voice, "I fell in love."

Isabella all but collapsed onto a wooden kitchen chair.

"Not you. Not you, Anna!"

"I fell in love." A sob broke from Anna's throat. "With the coldest, cruelest, most hard-hearted bastard in the world."

"What's his name?"

"Draco. Draco Valenti." Anna sank into a chair across from Isabella. "Prince Draco Valenti, no less."

"A handsome prince?"

"An ice prince. All sex, no heart."

"Wow. That's quite a description."

"It's accurate. But don't worry. I fell out of love fast enough. I mean, I realized how I really felt two minutes after I walked out on him. I'm just upset, is all. With myself, for having been such a jerk."

"Oh, honey…"

"Really. It's okay." Tears ran down her face as she looked at her sister. "I never actually loved him, Iz. I never would have. Never, not me, not in a billion years…"

Anna folded her arms on the scarred wooden table, laid down her head and sobbed.

* * *

Not too far away, in a much trendier part of Manhattan, in a bar that was still a bar and not a cocktail lounge or a club, Raffaele, Dante, Falco and Nicolo Orsini were having their usual Friday-night get-together.

The bar—actually, The Bar—was theirs, which was why it was still a bar despite the fact that the neighborhood, to their enormous distaste, had gone upscale.

Once, this had been the place where they shared talk of dangerous dilemmas and beautiful women.

Now they were all married. Very happily married, but they met anyway and talked sports and business, kids and family, and, yes, once in a while they even talked dangerous dilemmas.

Tonight they were talking about one of their sisters.

"Izzy agrees," Rafe said. "Something's up with Anna."

Nick bit into his burger, chewed, swallowed and nodded. "Yeah. But what?"

Falco lifted his beer to his mouth. "Isabella's going to try and find out."

"Could it be a man?" Dante said. His brothers

looked at him, and he sighed. "Right. Not our Anna. There's not a guy alive could bring our Anna down."

There was a sound from nearby. Somebody clearing his throat, maybe.

"Agreed," Rafe said. "A guy tried to upset our Anna, she'd take him out."

There it was. That same sound again. The four Orsinis looked up. A guy was standing next to their booth. He was big, like them. Dark haired, like them. Dressed in an expensive suit and handmade shoes, also like them, but his tie was crooked, his hair looked as if he'd combed it with his fingers and there was a glitter in his eyes that they all recognized as Trouble, definitely Trouble, and with a capital *T*.

The brothers looked at each other. *What the hell is this?* those looks said and, as one, they rose to their feet.

"Service is at the bar, pal," Falco said.

The guy nodded. Did that throat-clearing thing again.

"Listen," Rafe said, "you got a problem with the place or the food—"

"I am Draco Valenti," Draco blurted. "And she's not your Anna, she is mine."

Silence. A heavy, awful silence. Then Nick jerked his chin toward the door that led to The Bar's private office, and the five men marched to it, Draco surrounded by men he figured could grind him into dust if they decided that he was the problem, not the solution.

He could fight back. He was pretty sure he was as tough as they were, but there were four of them, one of him, and besides…

Besides, he had hurt his Anna. Their sister.

All things considered, if they wanted to beat the crap out of him, he wouldn't try to stop them.

A hand shoved him, none too gently, into a small, inexpensively furnished room. Desk. Phone. Chairs. And framed photos on the walls. Photos of these four. And of four smiling women. Babies. A toddler. A woman who had to be the mother of the clan. A slim, beautiful young woman with dark hair.

And Anna. His Anna, smiling and happy and lovely and—and God, how he missed her, yearned for her, needed her—

"So?"

Draco turned around. The Orsinis stood lined up, shoulder to shoulder, arms folded, jaws set. He was a fan of American football and he had a totally irrelevant thought.

He'd seen offensive linemen who looked less threatening than these guys.

"What do you mean, she's *your* Anna?"

He had no idea which of them had spoken the first time, which had spoken now. The only thing he did know was that now was not the time for introductions.

"You want it straight?" he said. "No bull?"

"Straight," one of them growled. "From the beginning."

So Draco told them.

Everything. Okay. Not everything. Not about what had happened on the flight to Rome, or what had happened in her hotel, or, *Cristo,* not what had happened in his bed.

But all the rest... He told them.

How he'd thought this was just going to be a weekend fling. One of them started forward when he said that, but the guy beside him muttered, "Cool it," and the other guy stood still the way a tiger might stand still before it made a kill.

Draco told them more.

He said that weekend fling hadn't been enough, how he'd convinced Anna to stay another week. How incredible the week had been, and how he'd suddenly realized he didn't want her to leave him when it ended.

Now came the hardest part.

He told them of the scheme he'd hatched. All of it. The job offer. The apartment. That what he wanted was to make Anna his mistress.

One of the Orsinis swung at him. He stood there and took the blow, straight to his jaw.

"Damnit, chill," one of Anna's brothers snarled, and glared first at Draco and then at the other three. "Been there, done that," the guy growled, and damned if the rest of them didn't sort of hang their heads.

"And now you're here," said the one who'd slugged him. "What took you so long?"

Draco had expected the question. His answer was blunt and honest.

"She said something that hurt me. About— about having been with other men."

"Let me get this straight," one Orsini said. "You're into a double standard?"

"No. I am not. It was only that—that by then Anna had made me forget every woman I'd ever known. To think that I had not done the same for her…"

"Yeah, okay. No need for specifics."

"I still don't get it. You think we're going to tell you that you can make our sister your mistress?"

Draco narrowed his eyes. It was one thing to be deferential, but quite another to be taken for a fool.

"If I wanted her to be my mistress," he said quietly, "I'd go to her, not you."

"Then what do you want?"

Draco took a breath. "Anna loves the four of you."

"Damned right. And we love her."

"I am Italian."

"If you think that makes this better—"

"I am also a prince."

"Whoopee," one of the brothers said, his tone flat and insulting.

"What I mean is that I carry a name that had once been respected." Hell. This wasn't going well. "But my father sullied that name, and I have spent my life trying to restore honor to it."

The atmosphere in the room eased, if only a little.

"Go on."

"You don't know the half," one of the brothers muttered.

"In Italy, honor demanded asking permission of a woman's family before asking for her hand in marriage."

A muscle twitched in one of those grim jaws.

"Is that why you're here? You want Anna to marry you, and us to tell her that she should?" Four deep, unpleasant barks of laughter. "If you knew anything about our sister, you'd know that nobody can tell her what to do."

"No," Draco said softly. "It's one of the things I love about her. I will do the asking, not any of you."

"And why should she say yes?"

"Because I adore her," Draco said gruffly. "And she loves me." Nothing. Not even a twitch. Draco narrowed his eyes. Eating crow was one thing; eating an entire rookery's worth was another. "I know that she loves me. It is the reason she acted as she did when she found out what I'd done."

"The bastard stood there," one of the brothers said grimly, "and watched her cry."

"She didn't cry. Another woman would have." Draco paused. "Anna hit me."

Silence. And then the Orsinis began to laugh. But as quickly as the laughter started, it stopped.

"Suppose we say no? Suppose we refuse you permission to marry her? Or even to ask her? Suppose we tell you to get the hell out of here and never look back? Then what?"

Enough, Draco thought, and he stood straighter, his dark eyes level with theirs.

"Then," he said quietly, "I am afraid I will have to take you on, one by one, and when I am the only one of us left standing—and I will be, in an honest fight—I will go to my Anna and put my life and my heart in her hands."

The silence that followed was surely the longest of Draco's life. Then Anna's brothers smiled. Grinned. Shook his hand and introduced themselves, and when the introductions were over, they wished him good luck and sent him on his way.

* * *

Autumn Peach was too dark, Russet Red was too deep and Pumpkin Patch was just plain insipid.

That was all Anna would talk about when she stopped crying, never mind Izzy's persistent questioning, and finally Izzy threw up her hands and said okay, fine, enough was enough. She'd go to the hardware store and get some more color samples.

"You're a pigheaded mule," she told Anna, and Anna tried to laugh at the impossible image, but she couldn't.

Laughing seemed out of the question.

At least she'd gotten rid of Izzy for a while. A half hour would give her time to regroup.

Unfortunately, Izzy had obviously decided leaving was a mistake, because the doorbell rang not five minutes later. Anna rubbed her eyes with her fists, pasted a smile on her face and went to the door.

"No," she said as she flung it open, "I will not compromise on Tangerine Twist...." The words died on her tongue. "Draco?" she said, and two things happened at once. Her hand balled into a fist so she could hit him, and Draco said her name and reached for her, and after a hesitation that surely lasted no more than a heartbeat, Anna sobbed her lover's name and went into his arms.

He kissed her, over and over. Her forehead. Her eyes. The tip of her nose. Her mouth. Oh, her mouth, even sweeter than he remembered.

"Anna," he said brokenly, "Anna, *bellissima, mio amante* Anna, *ti amo, ti adoro!*"

Anna didn't speak much Italian, but a woman didn't have to speak the language to understand any of those words.

"I love you, too," she whispered. "I adore you. I've missed you so terribly!"

"*Sì.* I have missed you, too. My heart, my life have been so empty…"

"That night," Anna said, "that awful night…"

"I was afraid to lose you. And afraid to try and keep you." Draco laughed as he framed her face in his hands. "I always thought love was a foolish fairy tale."

Anna smiled, even as tears rolled down her cheeks.

"I thought it was just a way of keeping a woman under a man's thumb."

Draco kissed her again.

"We were both wrong, *bellissima.*"

"Yes. Oh yes, we were."

Draco took a deep breath. And dropped to one knee.

"Anna. Beloved," he said, "will you do me the honor of becoming my wife?"

The smile that curved Anna's lips was, Draco knew, the most beautiful sight a man would ever see.

"Yes," she said, "oh, yes. I will."

He reached in his pocket, took out a ring and slipped it on her finger. It was a perfect copy of the Valenti crest, done in sapphires and diamonds.

Anna looked from her hand to her lover. Her eyes filled again.

"It's beautiful," she said softly. "And I am honored to wear it."

Draco rose to his feet. "Anna," he murmured, "*bella* Anna."

She went into his arms and he kissed her, kissed her until the world floated away. They never heard Isabella come in, never heard her hurried departure.

But when Izzy quietly shut the apartment door, she was smiling.

* * *

They were married two weeks later in the little church Anna's mother had always loved, on a street that was either part of Little Italy or Greenwich Village, depending on who you asked.

Sofia Orsini was thrilled with her new son-in-law, but she raised her eyebrows when he came to her at the party that followed in the observatory at the Orsini mansion and said he had a wedding gift for her.

It was the deed to the Sicilian land that sheltered the ruins of the castle that had belonged to his ancestors.

"Now it will belong to two families," he said.

Sofia shook her head and gently gave the document back to him. She said she had no idea what he was talking about, but that it was good to know her Anna had married a man who loved Sicily.

He shook hands with each of Anna's brothers, all of whom had been his best men— "Just try and talk me out of it," he'd told the wedding planner, who had not been foolish enough to try—and laughed with them in a way that told Anna they shared something, but none of them would tell her what it was.

He kissed his sisters-in-law, who had been Anna's bridesmaids, kissed the nephews and nieces he'd so suddenly acquired, and reserved a special hug for Anna's maid of honor.

"Isabella," he said, "Anna says you are the dearest sister a woman could possibly have."

"You next, kid," Rafe said to Izzy as he swept her away and danced her around the room.

"Right," Izzy said brightly, and thought, *Not me, not now, not ever in a million billion years.*

And, finally, he walked up to Cesare.

"Anna thinks she despises you," he said softly, "but the truth, *signore,* is that she loves you because you are her father." He looked the don straight in the eye. "And you made up all that nonsense about your wife's family and my land."

The don permitted himself a small smile.

"I may have had my facts confused. Anything is possible." He paused. "By the way," he continued, as if what he were about to say was unimportant, "I knew your father. He was not the best of men but then, neither am I."

Draco waited. Then he said, "And?"

The don smiled. "And, I suspect your father would be proud of the man you have become."

* * *

At last it was time for Anna and Draco to say goodbye and leave on their honeymoon.

They were flying to Venice, on his private plane. It was big and luxurious; the center aisle had been garlanded with white roses.

Draco carried his bride down that aisle to the private bedroom in the rear of the plane and kicked the door shut after him.

"This is how it all began, *cara,*" he said softly. "A plane. And you. And me."

Anna smiled as he set her slowly on her feet. She was wearing stilettos, of course. Still, she had to rise on tiptoe to kiss him, and then to put her lips to his ear and whisper something hot and wicked.

His eyes grew very, very dark. Slowly he shrugged off his jacket. Undid his tie. Unbuttoned his shirt.

"Anna," he said in a voice that was pure sex.

Anna laughed and wound her arms around his neck.

"Draco," she whispered. "What took you so long?"

* * * * *

Mills & Boon® Large Print
November 2011

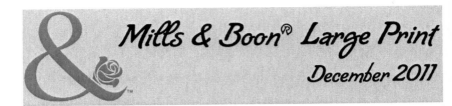
Mills & Boon® Large Print
December 2011

BRIDE FOR REAL
Lynne Graham

FROM DIRT TO DIAMONDS
Julia James

THE THORN IN HIS SIDE
Kim Lawrence

FIANCÉE FOR ONE NIGHT
Trish Morey

AUSTRALIA'S MAVERICK MILLIONAIRE
Margaret Way

RESCUED BY THE BROODING TYCOON
Lucy Gordon

SWEPT OFF HER STILETTOS
Fiona Harper

MR RIGHT THERE ALL ALONG
Jackie Braun